THE PILGRIM

THE
PILGRIM

DAVIS BUNN

Franciscan
MEDIA
Cincinnati, Ohio

This is a work of fiction. Names, characters, corporations, institutions, organizations, events, or locales in this novel are either the product of the author's imagination or, if real, used fictitiously. The resemblance of any character to actual persons (living or dead) is entirely coincidental.

Cover design by Candle Light Studios
Cover illustration by Candle Light Studios and Shutterstock
Book design by Mark Sullivan

LIBRARY OF CONGRESS CATALOGING-IN-PUBLICATION DATA
(from hardcover edition)
Bunn, T. Davis, 1952-
The pilgrim / Davis Bunn.
pages ; cm
ISBN 978-1-63253-034-9 (alk. paper)
I. Title.
PS3552.U4718P55 2015
813'.54—dc23
2015008016

ISBN 978-1-63253-034-9 (hardcover edition)
ISBN 978-1-61636-865-4 (paperback edition)

Published by Franciscan Media
28 W. Liberty St.
Cincinnati, OH 45202
www.FranciscanMedia.org

Printed in the United States of America.
Printed on acid-free paper.
15 16 17 18 19 5 4 3 2 1

This book is dedicated to my mother,
Rebecca Bunn;
my sisters,
Nancy Smith
and
Bunny Matthews,
with love and thanksgiving.

CHAPTER 1

H elena stood upon the ship's deck and surveyed the army sent to kill her.

Before her stretched the harbor of Judea's provincial capital, Caesarea. The city was rimmed by hills, and the hills were crowned by temples and palaces. The might of old Rome was firmly established here, and it was her enemy.

To the right of the harbor rose the arena, a great ring of stone and blood. On its left was the palace erected by Pontius Pilate three centuries earlier. The seaside palace of the governor of Judea was alive with lights. Oil lamps burned in almost every window, and torches lined the road leading down to the port. More lights rimmed the stone plaza fronting the docks, great metal urns raised upon tall pillars. They illuminated the men standing in ranks, ten centuries, a full legion. Their spears and shields and bronze helmets flickered ruddy and perilous in the flames.

She had yearned all her life to make this journey. And now that she had finally arrived, an army was ready to see she never left.

Helena had risen from innkeeper's daughter to wife of a caesar. But her husband had cast her aside, and in the eyes of Roman society she was now a woman disgraced. According to Roman custom, Helena was expected to hide away in shame. Instead, she had traveled to Judea, following the will of a God the Roman world had spent four centuries trying to wipe from human memory.

Even in her early life, Helena had known the importance of appearances. Her father's inn had any number of serving wenches, slatternly girls with brassy laughs and easy manners. Helena had needed to separate herself from them before she even opened her mouth. She had to ensure that none of the patrons ever thought for an instant about trying their way with her. She had made it a practice to keep her few things in good order. Her blond hair was always carefully done up, and her hands were clean. Each night she rubbed them down with goose fat to keep them from becoming rough and raw. The serving wenches called her uppity. But Helena knew she lived one small step away from joining them. The nightmare she most dreaded during her early years was hearing the wenches' saucy laughter coming from her own lips.

These were strange thoughts to be having as she joined her small company on the ship's foredeck. Especially now, when her appearance was stained by eleven months of travel. Not to mention the impact of being cast from her home and life and marriage by a husband who wished to spend his remaining days chasing young maids.

Helena forced herself back into the present moment. The young officer who had met them four days ago, just as their vessel was leaving the island of Cyprus, approached and saluted. Helena stifled the urge to order Anthony to stop with all such gestures. She knew he disapproved of her and of this journey. She also knew he carried some immense burden. Helena's son had mentioned this in the letter Anthony had delivered. Constantine hoped the quest would bring Anthony back to the land of the living. Despite his perpetual gloom, Anthony's presence remained a gift. Helena forced herself to smile and wish him a good morning.

His response was not so much sour as brooding. "Empress, the Judean officials are waiting."

"I have asked you not to call me that."

Anthony surely knew he was a handsome man. But he treated his looks as a burden. He fidgeted inside the uniform of a Roman centurion, adjusting his helmet, tugging at his sword-belt, clearly worried by what awaited them on the shore. "How am I to address you, then?"

"My name is Helena."

"Highness, using a royal's name is punishable by death."

"I no longer hold any title. Or office." As he well knew. "You may refer to me as mistress, or my lady."

"As you will, my lady." He risked a glance at her clothes. "Don't you intend to change clothes?"

She glanced down at the gray shift, the simple sandals, the cloth belt. They were the clothes of a poor commoner. Or a pilgrim. "This is what I intend to wear for the entire journey."

"My lady…"

"Speak freely. Now and throughout our trip."

"You are about to meet the royal provincial governor, who answers only to the caesar in Damascus."

"I am aware of who awaits me on the quayside. My son considers them both his enemies."

Anthony scowled at the legion massed along the harbor. "Which is all the more reason for us to withdraw to a safe port and send for more troops."

"We are not here to wage war, Anthony."

"My lady, I have no idea why we are here at all."

Her son had described the centurion as a good man who deserved better, wounded by life and love, and needing Helena's guidance more than any man Constantine had ever met. Helena asked, "And yet you accepted my son's request to act as his envoy?"

"I will serve Constantine with my dying breath."

That was so like her son's officers. Constantine's greatest gift was his ability to draw such loyalty from his men. "Let us hope it does not come to that."

Anthony stared over the waters at the troops. In that instant, Helena realized the man had not merely come to serve her son. There in the man's haunted gaze, she saw the truth.

The centurion had traveled with her to Judea in search of his grave.

Helena declared, "This will not do."

Reluctantly he turned back to her. "My lady?"

She would not have the blood of another man on her hands. To go with her because he recognized the call of God was one thing. To go seeking death...

She said, "My priest and friend throughout my disgrace caught a fever on the trip from Rome and died in Crete. I thought perhaps God wanted me to face this quest utterly alone, bereft of kin and allies. Then you arrived."

Anthony's brow furrowed in confusion. But more important, he also became focused fully on her, perhaps for the first time. He set aside both the enemy that waited on the shore and the burden he carried. He *listened*.

Helena pointed at the emblem stamped into his leather breastplate. "Do you know the meaning of this insignia?"

"The general, your son, he saw it emblazoned on the sun."

"He had a *vision*. Do you know what the Lord called him to do?"

"We all know. Everyone who fought with him that day."

She said it anyway. "God told my son to place this new symbol, made from the cross overlaid by the name of Jesus, upon a standard and carry it before him. And God would give him victory. Do you believe my son actually heard the voice of God?"

"I know he believed he did. I know we had a great victory, against an army ten times greater than our own. That is enough."

It wasn't, but no argument would change this young man's mind. That was up to God. "I too have had a vision. And on the very same dawn as my son. That is why I came. That is why my son has supported me, though he remains opposed to this journey. Constantine agreed. Reluctantly. And allowed me to travel as a simple pilgrim."

"God told you to do this?"

"He did."

"Without troops?"

"Exactly."

"My lady, you will perish."

"It is certainly possible."

"I don't...You came to die?"

She stepped in closer still. "I should be asking you that."

Anthony flinched, but he held her gaze. And did not respond.

She started to tell him what God had said, that she would not only survive this quest, but bring glory to the empire and the world beyond her ken. But something held her back. So she merely set her hand upon his arm and said quietly, "I came to do God's will. The question is, are you ready to join me in this quest? And do so for the right reason?"

: CHAPTER 2 :

:

Helena did not really want her world to end. She simply wanted it to be different.

It was a desire that had carried her through her childhood and early years. She had started this journey thinking that the quest would serve her well enough once more.

Only now, as she stood and watched their ship glide across oil-slick water, she was not so sure.

She could feel Anthony's tense disapproval. Which was hardly a surprise. He expected them all to die very soon. And then there was the manner of her dress. The simple garment of gray linen covered her from neck to ankles. She wore no jewelry, no badge of rank, no crown.

Like most of Constantine's officers, Anthony clearly regarded Helena's son with awe. Constantine, her only child, was thirty-two. He was the youngest Roman general in almost two hundred years. He was considered by many to be the finest military leader in the empire's history. Anthony did not say anything. But she could sense his brooding displeasure. Dressing like a commoner insulted her son and everything he stood for.

Helena said, "Describe what awaits us, if you would."

The ship glided slowly toward the quayside. Dockhands stood ready to catch the ship's lines and make it fast. Beyond them was massed the might of Rome. Anthony replied, "Judea is run from Damascus. Damascus is ruled by Caesar Maximinus. The man you see lounging beneath the canopy is his appointed governor, Firmilian. Maximinus and Firmilian are sworn enemies of all followers of Jesus. Their persecutions have been harsher than anywhere else in the empire. They scorn you and your son. Nothing would please them more than boasting that they had caused your death."

"It would certainly delight all my son's enemies," Helena agreed.

"Maximinus is not satisfied claiming the title of caesar in Damascus," Anthony went on. "He wants to be crowned ruler of Rome. Causing your death would bring that much closer. But he won't do it today."

Helena felt a faint rush of hope. "Why not?"

"Because it is too public. His enemies and your son's allies would declare him a murderer. He would lose the support he's building in the Senate." Anthony scowled at the soldiers standing at attention. "He'll wait until we are beyond the public eye. Then he will wipe us out."

The lines were tossed and the ship pulled in tight to the stone embankment. Overhead a gull passed, crying a forlorn welcome. The ship's captain shouted orders, and the gangplank rumbled out. Beyond the armies and the weapons and the officials and the arena rose the steep-sided hills. The temples were burnished by the rising sun, heightening Helena's sense of entering a realm from which there was no escape.

Helena knew the young officer expected her to express some concern, or fear, or at least a hint of strategy. And he deserved that much. All of those who traveled in her small group should understand why she was taking what they all thought was a suicidal risk.

She said, "I do not come to the Holy Land as a disgraced wife. I have no interest in holding onto titles and glory that my husband's actions have stripped away. I come to Judea as a pilgrim. I carry with me an eternal quest."

Anthony gestured to the array of armed men. "My lady, they care nothing about your reasons for coming. In their eyes, you are not just weak. You are prey."

Cratus, her grizzled guard-sergeant, grunted in agreement. Helena traveled with four guards and a maid, the wife of her former priest who had died. Helena's maid was the most silent woman she had ever known. They had scarcely exchanged a half-dozen words since setting sail. Cratus and his four guards stood with the stolid resignation of men who had spent the entire journey coming to terms with their fate.

Helena replied, "Which means we must rely on our Lord's strength to protect us."

Anthony was still working on his response when Helena bowed her farewell to the captain and walked through the ranks of sailors. Anthony sighed and followed her, the maid, and Cratus and his four guards. Helena's sandals made a quiet slap-slap down the gangplank.

The Caesarean legions were drawn up in perfect order along the stone dock. Beyond them rose the palanquin bearing the consul of Caesarea. The yellow silk canopy flapped in the morning breeze. Firmilian and his courtiers were rendered speechless by the sight of Helena disembarking.

Helena knelt by the gangplank, lowered her face to the stones, and kissed the dust. She had dreamed all her life of journeying to the Holy Land. But never had she imagined it might happen like this. Disgraced, cast aside, alone save for the company of strangers, facing enemies who wanted her dead.

She had nothing to rely upon but the promise of a God who felt very distant just then. Helena rose to her feet and softly declared, "And so it begins."

* * *

At a bellowed command, the troops stamped to attention. Their swords glinted in the sunlight like a forest of steel. Helena paid the soldiers no mind. Flanked by Anthony on one side and Cratus on her other, Helena walked down the central aisle. She halted in front of the palanquin and bowed as a humble servant. "It is kind of you to come and greet a simple pilgrim, Consul."

Firmilian was a corpulent toad in silk. His robe was the color of ripe lemons. His cheeks were so pudgy they pushed his little mouth into a permanent pout. He turned her title into an insult. "Augustine Helena."

"We both know that title is untrue, good sir."

"And yet your husband, the general, insists that the world address you as empress."

The bevy of officials clustered about the palanquin smirked at her. Helena knew the governor intended to shame her, make a public declaration of her many failings. So she raised her own voice and disarmed him. "My *former* husband has retired from all official duties."

"But...He still calls himself caesar of the north."

She did not shrug so much as lift her hands in helplessness. "The Senate has declared him officially retired. And I am no longer his wife. He divorced me."

The man shifted on his bed, causing the slave holding the near pole to flinch. Firmilian said, "But your son, Constantine, claims—"

"Forgive me, sire. Constantine is but a general. Nothing more. As we both know."

Firmilian searched for something to condemn. Or heap scorn upon. Which was proving impossible, since Helena stood before him in utter humility, claiming nothing whatsoever for herself. She might as well be a serving wench, which of course was how her son's enemies referred to her. Which added a bitter spice to the moment, as she addressed the governor like a humble penitent.

The consul's officials observed the exchange as they would a bit of good theater. They were easily ignored. But one man caught Helena's eye. He was as different from the rest as a hawk among gaudy songbirds. What was more, he knew it. He was dressed in the manner of a Roman officer, and yet there was something odd about him. It was more than the insolent way he eyed the officials. Nor was it merely his burnished uniform. Many Roman officers were granted breastplates of solid gold as reward for great victories. Most wore them only for grand formal occasions. Otherwise, they were kept on a special stand, like an armless statue, a centerpiece for all visitors to admire.

This man was different. He did not wear his gold breastplate to honor the consul or this occasion. He did it to be noticed. He *wanted* her to see him, to study his features, carved from some harsh desert stone. She was to observe the threat in those glittering black eyes and know that she was his prey.

He wanted Helena to be afraid.

Firmilian demanded, "What is your purpose here?"

She forced her gaze back to the governor. "I journey to Jerusalem. On pilgrimage."

The word *pilgrim* was not new. But the meaning had changed beyond all recognition. Before, pilgrims had been followers of the secret sects, the Greek mystery religions that demanded strict obedience. Now, a Christian pilgrim was one who gave feet to their prayers. They asked for a miracle, and they carried this prayer with them to a place of significance to the life of their Lord.

The fat man on the silk palanquin sneered. "So it's true, then. Your family has gone over to this Jesus."

"We have."

"Christians are banned. They are outlaws. Their crimes are punishable by death." He waved at the grand structures that crowned the ridgeline. "Rome is ruled by Roman gods."

Helena did not respond.

"Well, then." He made a moue of distaste. "I suppose you'll be wanting provisions. And transport. And to use the royal palaces."

"We want nothing."

This time he did not bother to hide his astonishment. "But... how will you travel? Where will you stay?"

"We journey on foot, as pilgrims should. We will camp. We will purchase our own provisions." She bowed more deeply still. "But I thank you for your offer of generosity."

He had made no such offer and flushed at the implied criticism. "You will find nothing between here and Jerusalem but desert bandits and death."

"Our God will provide."

"Where are your troops?"

"I have none." She swept a hand back to where her maid waited with Anthony, Cratus, and the four guards. "I travel only with these gathered here."

Helena knew the consul had expected their convoy to be filled with soldiers. Her son was general over all the armies of the west. Constantine's domain ran from the Danube to Hadrian's Wall, a region over a thousand miles wide. Of course, Firmilian had expected to greet a horde of armed troops. Which was why he had massed so many of his own soldiers. The man's laugh was a high-pitched cackle. "Then you will die!"

"That is in God's hands, Consul. Would you be so kind as to deliver a message to Damascus?"

"Perhaps. Who is it from?"

"My son. And Licinius."

The flat gaze tightened. Licinius was the general who ruled the eastern armies. He had recently allied himself with Constantine. Though Licinius did not share Constantine's faith in Jesus, he was the only other Roman general who did not count Christians as enemies.

The fact that Constantine claimed no political rank made the situation even more troubling for his enemies. Constantine fought any usurper who sought the throne of Rome. And yet he refused to claim it for himself. It was assumed by most that Constantine waited for the people to *ask* him to take on the role of supreme leader. But no one knew for certain, for the general himself refused to speak.

The consul gestured. "Very well, give me the letter."

Helena extracted the sealed parchment from the pocket of her robe. It had been brought to her by Anthony, who had no idea what he carried. Constantine had merely told the officer that the message he carried was urgent, that many lives depended upon him delivering it. "My son asks that you deliver this to Maximinus with all possible urgency. Once you have read it for yourself, of course, and can confirm just how urgent this document is."

Impatiently, he broke the seal and unfolded the note. "I will determine what is urgent..." The man's words failed as he read. "This is madness."

"It is the *law.*" Helena raised her voice so all the consul's retinue could hear. "Licinius has been appointed caesar of the east. He and my son the general have issued a joint edict declaring that Christians are to be restored as full Roman citizens."

"This cannot be." The corpulent man's fingers trembled violently, causing the parchment to flutter like a large white fan.

"All property confiscated from followers of Jesus will be *immediately* returned," Helena continued loudly. "All rights as Roman citizens are *immediately* restored. All churches that have been destroyed will be *immediately* rebuilt at the government's expense. Every imprisoned Christian is to be *immediately* freed."

"There will be chaos," the consul muttered.

"From this day forth, Christianity is no longer an outlaw religion." Helena shouted the words. "Any who treat it as such, or persecute believers, will be sentenced to death. This law, signed by your caesar, shall be known as the Edict of Milan."

"Madness!" Angrily Firmilian tossed the parchment aside. "Maximinus is caesar of the east!"

"Your Senate says otherwise."

"The Senate is over a thousand miles away. This paper is worthless. This audience is at an end." Firmilian gestured crossly. As the palanquin shifted around, the consul glanced at the man who stood isolated by more than the distance between them. Firmilian then tossed over his shoulder, "And your bones will soon bake beneath the desert sun."

: CHAPTER 3 :

:

As Helena crossed the city's main thoroughfare and headed for the arena, she found herself recalling the home she would never see again. The home from which she had been evicted by a squad of armed men. Led by Cratus. Who now served as her chief guard.

She had a dozen more important things to be thinking about. First on the list, of course, had to be the question of whether she would survive the next few days. But just then she was so filled with the old hurt she could scarcely see where she walked.

When Helena had met her husband, he had commanded the Roman region of west England. Soon after, he had been promoted to rule Dalmatia, a troubled province of warring tribes. Helena's husband had spent most of his time away, which was the life of most Roman officers. When he was home he had filled their life with rollicking laughter and a fierce love for their lone child, Constantine. Her husband had settled Helena in a hillside villa with a splendid view of the coastline and the sea. Their home had been built from the region's coarse granite and, by Roman standards, had been a modest affair. The region had suited her, for it was as rough and wild in nature as her homeland. But the weather had been far kinder, with cool sea winds all summer, and the hills had sheltered them from the worst of the winter storms. She had raised their son and welcomed her husband back from his many campaigns. And she had asked for nothing more out of life than what she had.

Until that day, eleven months earlier, when the troops had entered the courtyard.

Every military wife knew the dread of soldiers returning without her loved one among them. Helena had spent years fearing the messenger bearing a black wreath of widowhood. But nothing, no matter of time or circumstance, could have prepared her for that morning.

Helena had recognized the lead man, a grizzled veteran who had stayed in her family's guest lodgings several times in the past. "Cratus, is it?"

"Aye, highness. It is."

She took in his weary state, the mud and sweat covering the horses, and the near exhaustion of his troops. "Why don't you and your men enjoy the baths. I'll have the servants prepare a meal, then—"

"Highness, my news cannot wait."

She watched him slip from the horse's back and hoped her legs would manage to hold her aloft. "Speak, then."

"Perhaps we should move inside."

"Your men know the news?"

"Aye, highness. That is…"

She gripped the stone banister. "Tell me."

He had the grace to look genuinely pained. "You are divorced."

"I…What?"

"Your husband, that is, the general. He has divorced you." Cratus scowled fiercely at the horizon, as though searching for some enemy worthy of his wrath. "He orders you to leave."

"Go? From my home? But where am I…"

"Highness, your son has been informed. He invites you to join him."

Her mind felt sluggish, as though struggling against unseen currents, and losing. "My son and his army are fighting for their lives."

"Aye, it is grim going. But if anyone can survive, it is Constantine."

She found comfort in the old soldier's admiration. "How long do I have before I must depart?"

The scowl returned. "Only the hours you require."

They had been sent, she realized, to force her out if necessary. Helena fought off the bitter sorrow and said, "You and your men go and refresh yourselves."

Cratus found the entire affair very hard going. "Highness, we are ordered to help you make all possible haste."

"And so you shall. But first you must rest and bathe and have a proper meal." She forced herself to turn around and climb the front stairs and not wobble. She was, after all, a general's wife. Or had been, until that very day. "We leave tomorrow."

* * *

Helena's journey from her former home in Dalmatia to her son's headquarters in the southern Alps had taken over a month. By the time they arrived, she and Cratus had become fast friends. Helena's son had recognized their affection for one another and requested that Cratus become the master of her personal guards.

What Cratus might think of that duty now, when they both faced the very real threat of death upon the road to Jerusalem, she had no idea. She had warned him, of course. Cratus had responded that he had given his word to Constantine. He would defend her to his final breath. He considered the duty an honor. And he would be grateful if she did not question his loyalty again. It was the longest speech she had ever heard him make.

Where the main road joined with the avenue fronting the arena, she said to Cratus, "We need provisions for the journey. And mules to carry them."

"Horses are the thing, mistress. Mules make for a terrible jarring ride. By the end of the journey, we'll be hating the beasts."

"We might, if we planned to ride at all. Which I don't."

He rarely showed surprise at anything, this one. But he gaped at her now. "You can't mean you plan to walk. Not all the way."

"You heard what I told the consul. I come as a pilgrim. I shall walk."

"But mistress—"

"Buy whatever you want for yourself. A horse, a dozen horses, a chariot even. But I am walking." She ended the argument by turning to Anthony. "That man who stood with the courtiers but was not one of them. The Roman officer in the golden breastplate."

"I saw him. And he was no Roman by birth."

She liked his awareness and the blunt manner of speech. "What was he, then?"

"Your doom."

"You know him?"

"I know his kind. He's a trained killer."

She tried to remember her earlier vision, the peace, and failed. "That was my impression as well."

"Shall I find out what I can about him?"

"Does it matter?"

He gave a humorless smile. "Probably not."

She decided to repeat what she had told him at sunset the previous day. "You don't need to stay, Anthony."

He seemed genuinely surprised by her comment. "Haven't we already covered this ground?"

But she wanted to be absolutely certain of his decision. "You were sent as a messenger. You did as you were ordered. The letters have been delivered. You may go."

"My lady, your son asked me to make sure you were safe. I intend to do that as long as I am able."

"He *asked* you. He did not *order* this."

"Ask, order, it is all the same."

"Not for me, it isn't. And if I were to command you to leave?"

"My first loyalty rests with your son. I could not face him unless I knew I had done my best at his *request*."

Cratus lingered a step back, listening hard. He gave Anthony's response the tight approval of a subaltern for a superior officer who had measured up. Only then did the old soldier turn and walk away.

Helena nodded her acceptance and said, "Come with me."

: CHAPTER 4 :
:

As far as Anthony was concerned, everything about Constantine's mother left him uncertain. Anthony did not like uncertainty. The only thing he liked less was making mistakes in battle. Anthony had been a favorite among the troops because he valued them and their abilities and their lives. He was that rarest of breeds, an officer who led from the front. A trait he shared with Constantine.

As they descended the stairs that led to the bowels of the arena, Anthony said, "Might I ask what we are doing here, my lady?"

"We need a direction."

"I thought we were headed for Jerusalem." He almost added, "At least as far as our enemies allow us." But after learning they were going to walk, he knew the entire discussion was futile. Without horses, they would have no chance of escape when they were attacked. Which he assumed would happen as soon as they cleared the city's gates.

Helena merely said, "We need to make a stop along the way. I hope someone here will tell us where that is."

Anthony drew his short sword and used the pommel to hammer the steel gate. A few moments later, the barrier ground up. The senior jailer was a massive brute with a chest as big as an oak barrel. When the flame of his torch revealed an officer standing before him, he saluted with a fist to his chest. "You wish for something, sir?"

But it was Helena who answered, "You are holding Christians?"

Throughout the empire, arena jailers were disgraced legion-naires assigned this duty as punishment. The jailer and his motley crew remained in the dark stone chambers, blind to the crowds and the screams and the gaiety above, until their superiors deemed they had served their time. Many lived their remaining days in the dank cellars, as imprisoned as the unfortunates they sent upstairs to die.

The jailer took in Helena's simple dress and glanced uncertainly at Anthony, who ordered, "Answer the lady."

"The place is empty as the tomb at present, your honor. No games scheduled for a month and more."

"Where are they now, the followers of Jesus?" When he hesitated, Helena snapped, "Come, come, sir. I know full well the reputation of your masters. The governor in Damascus is notorious for hunting down believers and offering them up as fodder for the games."

The jailer used the torch to point south. "They're all held in the copper mines down the coast. Phaneao, the place is called."

"I expect the place holds a savage reputation," Helena said.

"There's some who say the prisoners beg for their day in the arena," the jailer confirmed. "At least they'll know an end to their woes."

"Then that is where we shall go." She started to turn away but then demanded, "What is your name, good sir?"

The jailer showed astonishment. Anthony could well understand why. Putrid fumes seeped through the open door, enveloping them where they stood. The jailer was filthy and held all the appeal of a cave troll. And yet this woman in homespun with a queen's bearing asked his name and called him sir. "Ianius, my lady."

"The Lord Jesus came to earth, Ianius, to bring light into your world. Give your life to him, and he will reward you with a hope that not even this vile place can extinguish. Mark well what I say." She turned to Anthony. "Come. Our duties lie elsewhere."

* * *

When they returned to the harbor, Cratus had seven mules lined up and provisions lashed to their backs. The veteran stood waiting at quayside while Helena and her silent maid went on board to fetch their belongings. Cratus asked Anthony, "There isn't a hope of her riding a horse, is there?"

"None at all."

"No. Thought not." Cratus squinted at the sunlit hills. "Suppose this is as good a place as any to die."

Anthony understood the unspoken component of this conversation. After joining Helena's company in Cyprus, Anthony had spent the voyage in relative isolation. Anthony was used to the ways of a tight-knit company, where outsiders were studied carefully before being admitted. Somewhere along the way, Cratus had decided to accept him into their ranks. "Why are you here?"

"I've been with the mistress since her divorce."

"I heard the rumors."

"Don't suppose there's anyone in Constantine's army who hasn't." Cratus described the day of their meeting in the offhand manner of a trooper delivering a report. "She responded as an empress should, that one. Not a tear, not a wail. Not even a word against the man who'd gone and shamed her before the whole world. By the time we made it to Constantine's camp, there was nowhere else I wanted to serve."

"Not even now?"

Cratus had the iron-hard gaze of a man who had stared death down a hundred times and more. "The lady led me to Jesus. Now she needs me. I am here for her. And for the Lord who leads us both."

"Did she tell you of her vision?"

"Only that our Lord had spoken to her. And that she should come here." Cratus squinted into the sun. "She has a general's way about her, that lady. She knows when to guard her words."

Anthony found himself liking the man a great deal. "When did you join up?"

"At sixteen. I was a ruffian, living hand to mouth on the streets of Milan. It was either sign up or starve. Yourself?"

"My father is a merchant supplying Constantine's army."

"Aye, I heard that somewhere. Sounds like a good enough life."

"It bored me to tears," Anthony admitted. "And I hate numbers worse than a punishment parade."

"That's a soldier's lot in life, I suppose. Misfits, one and all." He paused a moment and then asked, "His lordship asked you to stay on here?"

"Not exactly. What Constantine said was, 'See that she is safe.'"

"No one can do that. No one but the Lord of heaven. And even he may find his hands full on this trek." Cratus started to turn away but stopped and said, "Still and all, it's good to have you along."

Anthony was still looking for a response when Helena rejoined them. He watched as Cratus helped her and then the maid stow their belongings onto the last of the mules. The sergeant showed a gruff sort of affection as he lashed down their packs. It was fitting since he was helping the two women prepare for their final journey, showing them a fondness they were too distracted to notice. Anthony returned the salute of their vessel's skipper and then led their little band down the main thoroughfare, out of the port, past the arena, and through Caesarea.

Everywhere they went, people halted what they were doing and gaped at them. Soldiers, merchants, officials, citizens, slaves. The reaction was all the same. No one spoke. Even the children went quiet. Anthony tried to tell himself he didn't care. This woman who had once been almost a queen and was now reduced to walking the road in the gray cloth of a commoner's shroud, she had made her decision. Just as Anthony had made his. He grimly decided the most important thing was not to let himself be drawn in, not to care for these people. Because then it would be just too hard to let them die. Which they would. It was only a matter of hours. A few days at most.

As though in emphasis, Anthony caught the light glinting off a golden mirror. The officer who had mocked them now observed them from the hilltop temple of Jupiter. The assassin stood with arms on his hips, mocking them with his sneer and his stance.

Cratus moved up to walk beside Anthony. He held the mule's reins in his left hand, keeping his sword-hand free. He scowled in the direction of their enemy. "I asked the skipper about that one there. He's known as Severus and is Parthian by birth. He's the tame bandit of the caesar in Damascus."

"Maximinus is no caesar," Anthony replied. He had known men like Severus, who took pleasure in death. They were skilled artists at their craft and prized by leaders with more ambition than scruples. "And Severus won't attack us now."

Cratus grunted his agreement. "Don't give much for our chances once we're beyond the eyes of Caesarea."

Anthony forced himself to look away. He said, "If he gives me a chance, I'm going to challenge him to a duel."

"The man won't agree. I know his kind. He'll come at you quiet-like. If he is forced to attack straight on, he'll do so with ten times our numbers. He thumbs his nose at honor. He kills, and he moves on to kill again." Cratus shook his fist at the man on the ridge. "He'll show us no more regret than the leavings of his next meal."

Anthony tried telling himself that it was an honorable end. The fact that he was now being offered what he had spent the entire past year searching for should have left him, if not pleased, at least reconciled.

Instead, he found himself flooded by a biting sense of regret. As though he were letting someone down. Which was absurd, of course. The only life that had been crushed was his.

: CHAPTER 5 :

:

Caesarea had been planted with a military eye. The eastern hills formed a natural fortress that protected both the city and the harbor. Two winding valleys extended outward from the city's heart like outstretched arms. Anthony, Helena, and the rest of their small group departed through the southern passage and halted when they entered the Judean plains.

The valley broadened and flattened into the verdant green of carefully tended fields. A garrison fortress marked the point where the road met the plains, a hulk of stone and brute force that dominated the final hill. Merchants had established a caravan village beneath its protective shadow. Anthony decided to overnight here, for there was no telling where the next safe haven might be found.

A shepherd rented them use of a corral, which they shared with a merchant's convoy. Anthony and Cratus walked through the market, buying a few final items for the journey. A merchant warned them that the road to Phaneao was notoriously dry. Anthony purchased an additional beast to carry nothing but water skins and local fruit, which he bought as green as he could find.

For dinner, they roasted a goat stuffed with a local mixture of thyme and mint and coriander and rice. The seven of them ate almost the entire beast. It was the first fresh meat any of them had enjoyed since their ship had left Cyprus. Afterward, Helena retired to her tent. Anthony preferred to sleep under the stars so that all his senses could remain alert for any attack. He patrolled the perimeter as the brooding fortress faded into a silhouette. He halted by the merchant's camels, which he decided were the oddest animals on earth.

A voice from behind him asked, "Have you never seen a camel before, honored sir?"

Anthony turned to discover a beggar crouched just beyond the corral's fence. He was dressed in a filthy robe of indeterminate color. One eye was a dark hole. The other, however, showed a rare gleam. And he addressed Anthony in formal Latin.

Anthony replied, "Until this night, I have only seen drawings of the beasts."

"Then the honored sir has never visited Judea."

"This is my first journey east of Athens."

"Camels are truly miraculous creations. One of God's most astonishing feats, if you ask me." The man levered himself up. He limped and bore his weight upon a long staff. An injury to his left ankle had been poorly mended. "Camels can go for as long as twelve days without water, cover two hundred miles between drinks, and carry their own weight in goods."

"Do all beggars in Caesarea speak an educated Latin?"

Despite his rags and injuries, he carried himself with dignity. "Have I asked you for anything, honored sir?"

"Not yet."

"Then would you not say that to call me a beggar is premature?"

Anthony found himself smiling. "I wager you would not refuse an offer of food."

"How could any gentleman refuse such an invitation?"

"Wait here." Anthony crossed to their campfire and placed the remaining roasted meat on a clean platter. When he returned, the man squatted in the dirt by the animals. Anthony watched as he closed his good eye and bowed over the plate he cradled in his lap.

Anthony returned once more to their camp and brought a mug of tea back to the man. "There is no wine. The mistress forbids it."

"Then she is to be commended for her abstinence." The beggar ate and drank with almost delicate motions, as though trained to dine at a king's table. But the tremor to his fingers and the gauntness of his frame suggested a state of near starvation. "Might I inquire as to who this mistress is who leads your little band?"

"Are you a spy for the bandits?"

"Good sir, I am many things. But neither a spy nor a bandit are counted among them."

Anthony squatted in the dirt beside the man. "Where did you learn your Latin?"

"From the same source as you, I suspect. A tutor hired by my family, who pounded it into my thick skull." He cleaned his fingers on the edge of his robe. "Along with Greek, Hebrew, and a bit of Parthian that I have done my best to forget. Horrid tongue, Parthian. It suits the bandits whom you will no doubt soon encounter."

"And yet, here you are."

"A guest at your fine table," the man agreed and smiled. His teeth were brilliant, and his good eye showed undisguised humor. "As full as I have been in quite some time."

"There is more."

"I dare not eat another bite. But I would be happy to take whatever extra you have to share among those less fortunate." As Anthony rose to his feet, the beggar added, "And I would count myself in your debt if I might perhaps have a word with your mistress."

Anthony watched the stranger struggle to his feet. But when he offered a helping hand, it was waved away. "Why would any of my companions speak with this man who is not a beggar?"

"Some people consider my counsel to be of value." He rose
to full height for the first time, revealing himself to be as tall as
Anthony, who stood a full head higher than most men. "Especially
those who are headed into the reaches where you intend to travel.
That is, if your destination is indeed the city of God."

Anthony found himself facing a man whose dignity defied even
the rags and the filth. "Your name?"

"I am Macarius, bishop of Jerusalem." This time, his smile was
full of ancient woe. "A broken man leading a destroyed church in
a desecrated city."

* * *

Helena woke the next morning feeling very conflicted. Over the
past year, her life had become defined by loneliness. The friends
she had known in Dalmatia had all been taken from her, stolen
by the same divorce decree that had stripped away her home. She
had become close to an aging pastor traveling with Constantine's
army. But she had lost him to a fever on the journey from Italy.
Since then, she had not had anyone to talk to. Until the previous
night.

Helena found it perilously easy to reveal her fears and her
doubts to this stranger. Now in the morning light, she felt bitterly
ashamed by her weakness. At the highest realms of earthly power,
there was no meeting, no discussion, where the other person did
not have an aim, a desire, a purpose. She had all the experience
one person ever needed of that harsh truth. She threw back her
tent's flap, ready to face this so-called bishop in the light of a new
day and accept that she had again been manipulated.

Instead, by the time she finished sharing her breakfast with the
man, she found herself asking, "Would you join me in my tent?"

"Most certainly, highness."

"I would ask that you not call me that."

"And I should not have forced you to make such a request." He bowed over his crutch. "My lady."

Cratus demanded, "When are we to leave?"

"Soon. Pack everything but my tent." She held open the flap. "Please."

Once they were inside, she offered him the only chair, a folding campstool, but instead of accepting it, Macarius moved to the tent's other side and leaned upon his staff while she seated herself. Her maid stood by the tent-flap, there to observe without being fully present. Helena found the forbidden thoughts rising up with the intensity of a flood. "I fear I have only arrived here in Judea to disappoint my God."

"I doubt very much, my lady, that this is the case."

"Do you?" She told him about the morning that remained branded upon her mind and heart. The day Cratus appeared. The day her world and her life were shattered. She finished, "I never dishonored my husband. I never demanded expensive jewelry or a villa in Rome. All this was within my rights. I remained content to make a haven for my husband. A place he could return to and know safety and peace. Even when I heard the rumors about the way he lived when he was away, never did I rage or show him even an *instant* of bitterness or jealousy."

"You deserved better."

She found herself fighting against a sudden rush of tears. Which was absurd. She never wept. "I honored the sanctity of our vows. And how did he repay me?"

"He disgraced you before the world."

"In my heart, I am unable to forgive him. I say the words, and the act only makes me angrier. I wish he were disgraced and humiliated as he has made me. I wish…"

"You want him to pay. You want him punished. You want him branded and beaten and publicly scourged. You want him dead."

"It is terrible, isn't it?"

The scarred priest shrugged. "It is human."

"But God hasn't called me to be human. He has called me to a divine task. What if we fail because of my anger? What if I cause everyone who walks with me to die?"

Macarius gripped his staff with both hands and kneaded the wood between his fingers. The wood there had become polished and smooth. "The man who wears the golden breastplate. You know of whom I speak?"

"Severus." She wiped her face. "I saw him. Anthony calls him an assassin."

"He is that and more. He led the assault on the believers of Jerusalem. He slaughtered my flock with the careless ease of a man swatting flies. He tore down our church. He took from me my wife and my daughter. The two lights of my heart were lost to his knife."

"I'm so sorry."

"He watched me as he killed them, Severus did. And he smiled. As though my pain was his greatest joy. And then he used the same knife to inflict these wounds. Mixing my blood—"

"Stop. Please."

"My lady, you are not the only one who carries the burden of failing our Lord. I know I should forgive this man. I know it is part of my calling. And yet..."

For some reason, the words became the permission she required. Helena bowed over her knees and wept.

Macarius continued to knead his staff. "We are human, you and I. Imperfect vessels called to do the impossible."

She said into her hands, "What am I to do?"

"The same as I, my lady. The same as all mankind. We are called to do the best we possibly can. And trust God to do the rest."

: CHAPTER 6 :

:

Throw word 'bishop' comes from the Greek word for super-visor," Macarius explained as they set off down the southern road. "After the apostles all passed away, the various churches needed a senior elder or deacon who could speak for all the believers of that community. They were chosen as the final apostle had been, by prayer and fasting, followed by either choosing lots or casting votes."

Anthony knew that already but did not mind the bishop's easy conversation. Macarius was dressed in a new gray robe, a gift from Helena when he agreed to accompany them. He rode a donkey in jaunty good cheer. Anthony said, "You do realize that you are most likely traveling to your death."

The man replied airily, "If I feared death, young lad, I would have never agreed to lead the Jerusalem community. You know the decree of Diocletian?"

"Yes." The last emperor but one, Diocletian, had been the greatest enemy Christianity had ever known. Other emperors had hunted the Jesus community for amusement or sport, the worst of those being Nero. But Diocletian had gone much further. Early in his reign, Diocletian issued a decree condemning every Christian in the Roman world to death or enslavement. All churches were to be burned. All property was confiscated. The punishment was extended to every member of a believer's family, including infants. No one was to be spared. No punishment was deemed too brutal.

Macarius said, "These days, Diocletian's greatest devotees are Firmilian, governor of Judea, and Maximinus, ruler of Damascus. They are both slaves to pleasure. They delight in watching Christians suffer. It signals that they are right and we are wrong."

"Which is why," Anthony said, "you are committing suicide to travel with us."

"You are wrong, young lad," Macarius said cheerfully. "You are wrong."

"The assassin will wait until we are deep in those hills up ahead," Anthony predicted. "Then he will slaughter us. Down to the last man and beast. Firmilian and Maximinus will claim that Constantine's edict never arrived. And they will remain free to do whatever they please."

"You are forgetting one thing."

"And that is?"

Macarius gave him an impish smile. "The power of miracles."

Anthony's gaze was caught by a woman tending the fields through which their road passed. The road was built in Roman fashion. This close to the capital it was as carefully maintained as the fields, smoothly paved and elevated to reduce flooding. Anthony watched the woman harvest ripe turnips and dump them in the wicker basket by her feet. His gaze tightened upon the baby strapped to her back. As the woman moved, the sun tickled the baby's face. The infant waved its hands, trying to catch the sunlight whenever it appeared, and made a cooing sound over its game. Anthony thought of another wife and infant child, both lost to him. He shook his head against the bitter regret and said, "I know all about praying for miracles that never come."

Anthony walked away from the bishop, passing the string of pack animals, up to where the old guard walked alone. Cratus was in his fifties and possessed a strength that defied his years. The guard's nostrils were flared like a war-horse. He aimed them at the road ahead and breathed deep. "I smell blood that ain't yet spilt."

Anthony did his best to ignore the young mother and happy infant and studied the terrain. To either side of the road stretched seas of verdant green. It was May, and the spring harvest was now upon them. The fields were busy, and Anthony breathed in wood smoke and animals and tilled earth and fresh spices. There must have also been an orchard somewhere to his left, because the scent of blossoms came with every puff of easterly breeze.

Cratus demanded, "You think I'm wrong?"

Anthony hesitated and then decided there was no reason not to respond. "I fear you are right."

"I hope and pray the lady Helena's right about the miracles we've got in store."

"Macarius agrees with her, for what that is worth."

"He's an odd bird for a beggar." The veteran glanced back. Anthony did likewise and found that Helena had taken Anthony's place, walking beside the priest's donkey and talking earnestly. Macarius responded to their glances with a cheery wave of the hand not holding the reins. Cratus asked, "You believe what he said, about being a bishop and all?"

"I suppose I do, yes."

"So does Helena." Cratus rubbed one battle-hardened hand over the sword's pommel. "If I was the enemy, you know where I'd strike?"

"Yes." Anthony pointed to where the road began a snaking climb up hills to the south. "Right after the first curve, where the road vanishes behind those boulders."

The former sergeant sniffed the wind once more and then spat to leeward. "Ain't much we can do, not with six armed men and a cripple. Nothing but fight to the last and die as Roman soldiers should."

* * *

It seemed to Helena the southern hills mocked them all day long. Though they walked for hours, the ridgeline grew no closer. The air was very clear and the wind blew off the land, which kept the sea's freshness at a distance. By mid-afternoon, the heat was a blanket spread across the plains. Every muscle in Helena's body complained. She had spent six weeks at sea, and the absence of exercise was telling. She could feel Anthony's eyes upon her, so she did her best to hide her exhaustion. But finally, he moved up beside her and said, "Perhaps we should request the hospitality of one of these farms, my lady. Cratus smells danger up ahead. As do I. There is no need to rush into death's embrace."

"Our God will provide." Helena glanced behind them and could no longer see the tower guarding the entrance to Caesarea. The road ran arrow-straight north until it was swallowed by the afternoon haze. She turned back to find Anthony waiting for her response. She told him, "I will sleep under no man's roof until my pilgrimage is completed."

He nodded acceptance. "We can request permission to camp in their forecourt."

"Very well."

Anthony left the road and approached the nearest farm. He called back up, "The house and barns are empty."

Cratus searched around them. "As are the surrounding fields."

Anthony clambered back up the rise to stand alongside the guard-sergeant. "There isn't a soul to be seen."

Helena surveyed the empty vista. Two buzzards circled far overhead. She heard the bleating of sheep but could not see any animals. "Have they run away?"

"Not from us, you can be certain of that." The leather binding of the sergeant's sword-handle creaked beneath his grip. "More than likely they spotted the force that's been sent against us."

"This courtyard makes as good a campsite as we're likely to

find," Anthony decided. "The farm buildings will grant us protection. There's water, fresh fodder, and fruit on the trees in that orchard. We'll rest here."

Now that she had allowed herself to halt, Helena's exhaustion almost overwhelmed her. She staggered into the central courtyard as Anthony and Cratus searched the surrounding buildings. She found a sheltered spot beneath the farmhouse's overhanging roof and threw herself to the dusty earth. In an instant, she was gone.

* * *

Helena woke near dusk as hungry as she had been in her entire life. The need for more sleep was an ache in her bones. She rose slowly and discovered that her companions had erected the tent around her. She had noticed nothing. When she emerged, her silent maid handed her a tin plate filled with roasted lamb. Helena watched as Cratus baked flatbread on the stones lining the fire. He used his dagger to lift one and settle it on her plate. Helena had dined in palaces and eaten off the gold plates of princes. But never had she enjoyed as fine a meal as this.

She was on her second cup of sweetened tea when Anthony barked a warning.

She stood with the others and saw a group of perhaps a dozen soldiers hustle down the road toward them. They came from the north, the direction of Caesarea. The men huffed softly in the manner of troopers who had run themselves to the point of exhaustion.

Cratus inserted himself between her and the approaching threat. Helena could only assume that Firmilian, the consul in Caesarea, had sent a squad out to kill them. Cratus and the four guards unsheathed their weapons. The sound of the metal blades sliding from their scabbards left her trembling. Was this to be her last hour, before she and her friends were wiped from the earth and their ashes spread across the silent fields? She wanted to pray. But no thought came to her, no word. Only fear. It was one thing to seek death from a distance, but it was another thing entirely to stare directly into its dark maw.

Anthony stood above them on the road. What one man could do against a bevy of troops, Helena had no idea. Then he slowly straightened from his fighter's crouch. "Hold steady."

Cratus called up, "What is it?"

"Something is not..."

Helena noticed it too. There was no order to their march. In fact, they did not march at all. They stumbled, and they faltered. If they had not been wearing the leather breastplates of Roman soldiers, Helena might have assumed they were brigands.

Cratus asked, "Deserters?"

Anthony shrugged. "Why would they come here?"

Her fear lessened enough for Helena to count them now that they were nearer. They were nine in number. Their legs were white with dust from a long march, their features taut with exhaustion and something more. It was pain, Helena decided. The soldiers carried themselves as though they shared a singular agony.

Cratus said, "Perhaps they are a diversion."

"No need," Anthony replied, not taking his eyes from the band. "A cohort of trained legionnaires could wipe us out."

As they approached, their shared agony became ever more apparent. Their features were taut, their eyes hollowed. Most walked empty-handed. Some carried spears, but they held them with the tips pointed toward the earth, the Roman signal for peaceful intention. Helena knew a Roman soldier could lie like any other warrior, but Anthony was right, why should they bother? With their every step along the empty road, the more certain Helena became that she faced no threat from these men.

When they were ten paces away, Anthony lifted his hand. The men came to a halt. Anthony asked, "Who is your leader?"

The man who replied was a hardened veteran with scars on his shoulder and sword-arm and neck. "We have none."

Anthony asked, "Why are you here?"

Their spokesman licked dry lips. "The empress Helena travels with you?"

Anthony glanced down to where Helena stood beside the road. "She has commanded us to use no such title. She is simply Helena."

The soldier's words carried a raw desperation. "May we speak with her?"

Macarius limped forward, leaning heavily on his staff. "What possible business could you have with the mother of Constantine?"

There was no haughtiness to the spokesman's voice as he asked, "Who do I address?"

At a gesture from the priest, Cratus helped Macarius climb up to the road. "I am Macarius, bishop of Jerusalem. And I ask you again. What business is it of yours whom we travel with?"

"Are the legends true, that the empress brought her son to the Lord?"

"It is."

"And that Constantine now invites his men to pray to Jesus?"

Helena decided it was time to join her companions on the road. The men showed her no recognition. Why should they, facing a woman dressed in the simple gray robe of a commoner?

She heard Macarius reply, "That too, is true, though I have not seen it for myself. Now enough of your questions. Answer one of mine, or be gone. Why are you here?"

The veteran's voice broke over the simple words, "We have no place else to go."

The wind drifted about them, small puffs that pushed the hair across Anthony's forehead. Helena heard sheep bleat from some hidden corral and thought perhaps she also heard a child's cry. A songbird chirped a greeting to the setting sun. Other than that, the crowded road was silent.

"I am Helena, mother of Constantine." She stepped forward to stand beside Anthony. "Everything you have heard of my son and his armies is true."

The scarred veteran dropped to his knees. Swift as falling stones, he was joined by every other soldier facing them. "We come to ask your forgiveness, Augustine."

For once, she did not object to the title. "Your name?"

"Evander, your highness."

"Rise, Evander, you and your men."

"They are not my men, majesty." The soldier remained as he was.

"Why will you not stand before me?"

The man's jaw was knotted so tight it bunched the muscles of his neck and shoulders down to where they strained against the breastplate. "I dare not."

Macarius limped up to stand beside Helena. "My lady, perhaps I might be of service?"

"Speak."

He addressed the kneeling soldiers. "You are all believers, yes? And yet all of you publicly renounced your God?"

Evander's voice was branded with shame. "We have." The other soldiers' only response was to bow their heads more deeply.

Macarius explained, "All the armies of the Levant were ordered to offer libations to the Roman deities. Those who did not were first publicly tortured and then killed. The same fate awaited their families, to the youngest infant."

"I know of this." She moved closer to the men kneeling in the road's dust. "Evander, I order you to rise."

The man started to obey, but the strength suddenly left him. He sprawled face down in the dust. And groaned.

Helena knelt in the dust beside him. She gripped his shoulders and said gently, "You are commanded to rise."

With enormous effort, the man did as he was told. Tears streaked the white dust that covered his features. None of the other soldiers moved.

Helena said, "You do not bow before me. For I am nothing. I am a woman on a pilgrimage, without title or husband or home. I am a sinner. Just like you. One who has failed her God more often than I should ever care to count or recall."

"The things I have done," the soldier wept. The words were torn from his throat. "The innocents I have killed."

"You carry your burdens. I carry mine. And now you know why Jesus died upon the cross." Helena gave that a moment before saying, "Look at me, I implore you."

This time, all the faces rose to meet her, streaked by tears no soldier should ever shed. She asked, "Will you join with me? Shall we gather together as a family of believers and confess our sins to the One who died to free us of all pain?"

"I do not deserve this."

"None of us ever do." Her voice was gentled by the weakness she had just found within herself. "Macarius, will you assist us?"

He bowed. "My lady, it would be my honor."

CHAPTER 7

As the sunset dimmed, a wind rose off the sea. Their torches flickered and hissed. The wind was not cold, yet Helena could not stop the tremors that coursed through her frame.

They gathered in the empty barn. The odors of animals served as their incense. Macarius used a carpenter's table for an altar. Helena spread her cloak as a mantle over the scarred wood. At a gesture from the priest, Anthony filled one of their battered cups from the water skin. Cratus used his soldier's knife to cut pieces from his flatbread. Evander and the other soldiers knelt together, their shoulders touching, as any good Roman trooper was trained to do in the face of peril.

Helena found herself trapped in memories. She recalled the bitter fury she had known for her husband. Yes, she had every right to hate him. Yes, he had wronged her in ways beyond counting. Yes, she wept only in the isolation of her tent. Yes, all her secret thoughts had remained deeply hidden, even from her son. And yet, here in this Judean barn, she felt so ashamed of herself that she had to fight against the desire to kneel alongside the soldiers.

Macarius raised both cup and bread to the rafters and spoke a brief prayer. He then set down the bread and limped over to stand before the kneeling soldiers. He waited there in silence. Helena was certain the man would have waited there all night, if necessary.

When Evander lifted his gaze, Macarius said, "Will you and your men rise and stand before me?"

Reluctantly, the officer stood and motioned for his men to do the same.

Macarius gestured to the empty eye socket and to his scarred ankle. "Did you do this to me?"

Evander gripped his middle with both arms, the agony turning him rigid. "I might as well have."

"That is the right answer. Now listen carefully. You and all your men." He barked at them, "Look at me! Look!"

"Do as he says," Helena softly commanded.

Macarius stepped in closer still. The soldiers bowed back, as though linked in a shield wall and facing an onslaught of spears and swords. But they did not give.

Macarius said, "What say you, Evander?"

The words were drenched in the acid of misery and remorse. "Forgive me!"

"Again, you have answered rightly." The pastor lifted the cup and said, "On the night that our Lord was to be given up, he gathered with his disciples and shared with them the loaf and the cup. He said to them, 'This cup is the new covenant in my blood, which is poured out for you.'"

The officer whispered, "I cannot."

"Is your betrayal any worse than Peter's?" He offered the cup. "Take and drink."

Evander's hands shook so hard the liquid sloshed over them. He drank and then handed it to the next man. On around the group it went. Then Macarius took back the cup and carried it first to Anthony, then the others, and finally to Helena, who held it as Macarius himself drank.

Macarius set down the cup, picked up the bread, and said, "Only those who are aware of how far they have fallen can understand our Lord's gift. Only those whose regret is real, who have turned from their sins, who have begged for the impossible gift of forgiveness, can fathom the infinite mercy of God."

He blessed the bread and said, "Take this, each of you, and know that God's forgiveness will illuminate the days to come."

* * *

Following the Eucharist in the barn, Anthony fed Evander and his men the rest of the roast lamb before ordering them to lay down and get some rest. He patrolled once with Cratus, who had resumed his gloomy inspections of the hills that awaited them. For some reason, however, Anthony was freed of his concerns. His watch done, he lay down and slept better than he had since joining Helena.

The next morning, he awoke to find Evander and the other legionnaires had vanished.

Anthony did not believe it, not even when he stood over the space where the soldiers had slept. The only sign of the nine men was the indentation where they had lain.

Cratus came over to stand beside him. "I never would have taken them for cowards."

Anthony asked, "You noticed nothing amiss during your watch?"

"They clustered by the fire and talked. One of them asked our destination. I saw nothing wrong in telling them."

Anthony saw the guard-sergeant's worried frown and said, "There was no reason not to say. I would have told them myself."

Cratus breathed more easily. "An hour later, I returned from walking the perimeter, and they were gone."

"Why didn't you wake me?"

"What could you do? Run after them and beg?" Cratus squinted at the southern hills. "They are gone, and we are lost."

"Why would they leave?" Anthony kicked a fence post. "The empress did everything to make them welcome."

Cratus spat into the damp wind. "I followed their spoor. They headed south along the road, into the hills."

Which meant the soldiers headed in the same direction Helena intended to take. If Evander carried word to their enemy, they would soon be trapped. Anthony stomped about the camp, angry with himself for giving in to hope.

Macarius observed him with the smile of a happy man. He waved a hand at the sky, grim and gray as slate, and said, "It was on just such a day that the first believers gathered upon Golgotha and watched as the Messiah was nailed to the wood and hung upon the cross of shame. What they did not know, what they could not imagine, was that their tragedy forged the path home for all mankind. Now more than ever is a time for hope."

Anthony glared at the man, searching vainly for some bitter riposte. But his ill temper only seemed to brighten the priest's mood, who went on, "Out of just such dark times come miracles that shout to us across the ages: Hope! Joy! Peace!"

Anthony turned and stared south to where the road rose and curved and vanished. The desert colors were faded to match the sky. The southern hills were as hostile as fangs. He tried to tell himself that this was what he had hoped to find, a foe so great as to extinguish his life.

"Come join me, Anthony." Macarius motioned at the breakfast laid out on the trestle by the fire. "There is fruit and bread and cheese and tea. Fill yourself a plate."

"Where is Helena?"

"She sleeps. Let her. It will be a long day. Cratus, be a good man and pour the centurion a mug."

Anthony could find no reason to refuse. Once he was seated with the plate on his legs, he discovered he was famished. Macarius watched him eat with a parent's approval and did not speak again until he set the plate aside. "Tell me what it is that has you so angry with God."

The question was no less piercing for the gentle manner in which the priest spoke. Anthony drank from his mug but tasted only ashes.

"I have watched you closely, and I see a man who has forgotten how to smile. I see an anger that you carry like an old cloak, one not made for your shoulders."

Anthony asked sourly, "When in this world do we choose the burdens we carry?"

"Rarely, if ever," Macarius agreed.

Anthony realized the man had no intention of asking anything further. Nor, he sensed, would Macarius ever ask again. He told himself he had no interest in ever divulging the secrets he carried. And yet the words rose up inside him, the urge so powerful he could not hold them inside. "Her name was Rachel."

"She was what to you?"

"Wife. She died giving birth to our son."

"You lost your beloved and your firstborn. How terrible. When was this?"

"A Sabbath dawn. Ten months and three weeks back." Anthony felt again that horrid, cold wind, a blade that had cut deep as he dug the graves himself. He stared at the gray hills and recalled the only time he had held his son, when he lay him in the earth. He wished he had not spoken now, for he would need all his strength before this day was out. "It's hard to see God's hand in anything these days."

"Even last night?"

Anthony pointed to where the soldiers had lain. "All I see is no one to guard our flank."

"Then I pray that God will change your vision, Centurion. For I see us surrounded by miracles. And up there, in the hills you and Cratus study with such concern, I am certain that God's hand will show us more wonders still."

Macarius settled his hand upon Anthony's shoulder. It took him a moment to realize the man prayed for him. Anthony tried to refocus upon the hills and the coming threat. But the weight of the man's hand cast a veil over his senses, as though his prayers held the power to cause reality to fade. Anthony endured the man's concern as he would a coming blow, for such a day as this held no room for tears.

: CHAPTER 8 :

:

Helena had never considered herself a fickle woman until that morning. She awoke to a remarkable sense of calm. She held to this peace all through breakfast, even when speaking with Anthony and Cratus about the vanished men. And yet, as they broke camp and clambered back up to the road, she felt the calm flit away at that first glimpse of the southern hills. All it took was that one glimpse, and the warnings and the terrors were right there again.

The wind died as they started south, but the day did not clear. Nor did it rain. They walked the road beneath a sky the color of old iron. The farming valley was empty and vast and still. Helena had known such quiet before, when the local populace fled before armies. But usually, the people ran away from thrumping drums and harsh voices and spears that rose into the dawn like an evil forest. She traveled with one maid and five guards and a crippled pastor and Anthony. For Helena, the silence held portents of doom to come. A hawk circled high overhead, its cry a piercing farewell. She shivered anew and wished she had the strength to hold onto promises that seemed so far away.

Roman engineers built their roads in a straight line. They gave in to the dictates of nature with great reluctance. The road rose to meet the hills at a steady incline. The natural curves had been smoothed out, and where the ground dipped away, the engineers and their servants had erected a series of land bridges.

Anthony sped up until he was moving at the army's traditional marching pace, one half-step off a full trot. Helena knew that a good solider could hold to this pace for a day, sleep a few hours, do the same for three days longer, and then enter straight into battle. And Anthony was a good soldier indeed. One of the best. He had to be to serve on her son's inner council at such a young age. As he moved forward, Helena quaked at the thought of losing him to the unseen foes. She noticed the grim manner in which Cratus watched and realized that her guards all knew what Anthony intended.

He was offering himself as a sacrifice.

She called out to him and then regretted it instantly. Anthony neither looked back nor responded. Cratus and the guards remained silent. There was nothing to say.

Macarius moved up beside her and settled the hand not holding his staff upon her shoulder. She knew he was praying, just as he had earlier with Anthony. She watched the empty road and joined him in silent entreaty. For Anthony. For them all.

* * *

Anthony felt the drumbeat of hooves through his sandals before he actually heard anything at all.

He drew his sword and stationed himself in the middle of the road. Dust rose in the still air, tight clumps punched from the road by shod hooves. Anthony heard the horse wheeze in the manner of a beast that had been pushed to the limits of its strength and beyond.

When the figure appeared, Anthony discovered that it was not an attacker at all. Instead, he faced a Roman scout. The horse was so lathered that the foam covered its bits and bridles. When the scout drew on the reins, the horse faltered and appeared ready to buckle. "Steady, lass, steady!"

The officer leapt down, and his own legs proved no sturdier than those of his horse. The leather breastplate was drenched almost black with his sweat. His uniform was stained with dust and perspiration. He patted his horse's flank, waiting until he was certain the horse would remain upright. Then he turned and asked, "You accompany the empress?"

"I do." Anthony heard the tremor in his voice. "And you are?"

"Favian. Lieutenant in the ninth. Or I was." Favian spoke with the nasal drawl of a high-born Roman. The proper name for scouts was *speculatores*. Well-educated and meant to gather intelligence, they were typically assigned to the First Cohort, the elite troops of every legion. "So all is as Evander claimed, Constantine's mother has come to Judea on pilgrimage?"

"She has." Anthony found it difficult to release his tense muscles and straighten. "You used to scout for the ninth legion, but what about now?"

"Like the other Christian legionnaires who chose to live with dishonor, I poured my libation on the stones, made a false oath of allegiance to a god I did not believe in, and was reassigned to the mines." He untied the water skin. "Would you do me the service?"

Anthony uncorked the mouth and poured water into the scout's cupped hands. He liked how Favian saw to his horse before himself. The officer then accepted the skin, drank deeply, and went on, "I feared we would not arrive in time. The hill bandits have been marshaled by a man we have come to despise. His name is Severus."

"He stood beside Firmilian when we landed."

"He serves as the governor's pet assassin. I would rather sleep with a viper coiled around my neck."

"We expected to be ambushed in these hills."

"And you were correct." Favian paused to drink again. Tremors sent water cascading down his chest. He wiped his mouth and continued, "My men and I make forays along this route only once a month. It's hardly more than exercise for our mounts. The bandits see us coming and hide in the hills until we have passed. Only, this time, we captured a pair who came too close to our patrol. They confessed that Severus had ordered them to hunt out the empress."

"How did you find us?"

"We've been out here for three days and were heading back to Phaneao at dawn. Evander spied us just as we were breaking camp. My beast hasn't been called to such speed for years. The rest of my men follow on foot. We loaned our mounts to Evander." He patted the horse's flank. "To run into Evander on this empty stretch of road, in the first light of a day this grim, it was…"

"A miracle," Anthony muttered.

"It's true what Evander told us? The empress shares the sacraments to men like us?"

Anthony turned around. "Come and see."

* * *

When Anthony reappeared around the road's curve, walking alongside another Roman officer leading a weary horse, Macarius began to sing.

It was not much of a tune, for Macarius had no voice to speak of. But Helena recognized the hymn, and for one giddy moment, she found herself wanting to sing with him. Then she saw the flash of Anthony's teeth and realized it was the first time she had ever seen the man smile.

As the two men approached, she heard the officer who led the exhausted horse ask, "Where is the Augustine?"

"The lady in gray. But you would be well advised not to call her that."

The man's features were drawn and streaked with dust and sweat. "How am I to address her?"

"My lady. She has left everything behind. Including titles."

Helena heard the matter-of-fact way that Anthony spoke and was determined to find some way to thank him. Then the exhausted officer dropped to one knee before her and said, "I bring greetings, my lady, from the lost souls of Phaneao."

"Your name, sir?"

"Favian, my lady."

"Rise, good sir. And tell me what brings you here."

Anthony replied, "Favian is a scout. He and his men were on patrol when Evander's group met them in the highland valley."

"I don't understand," Helena said. "Evander left us to find you?"

"He had no way of knowing we would be there, my lady. He was on his way to the mines."

"How far are they from here?"

"A day and a night at a hard run."

"Evander was going to run to Phaneao?"

"He knew you entered the valley unprotected, my lady. He was going for help. He found us as we were completing our patrol. We gave him all our horses but this one. Evander and his men were exhausted, and we hoped they could now outrun Severus if he attacked."

Helena heard the priest murmur, "Miracle upon miracle."

But the priest's words could not extinguish her chill of fear. "You have seen this Severus?"

"We captured two bandits serving as his spies. They confirmed Severus is hunting you."

Cratus demanded, "A Roman officer is allied with hill bandits?"

"Severus is Parthian by birth," Anthony reminded him.

"He was a mercenary before he became an officer," Favian added sourly. "He serves the consul for gold."

She asked, "You are assigned to the mines?"

"For nine months now. Before that, I was chief scout for the Damascus legion."

"You lost your position because of your faith?"

"I bowed before the stone gods." His shame bent his head. "I take small comfort in having saved my two daughters from the slaughter."

Anthony said to the dust at his feet, "If it had been my children under threat, I would have sworn allegiance to the moon and stars."

The only sign that the scout heard Anthony was a slight straightening of his shoulders. "My men should be joining us by tomorrow's dawn, my lady. Evander should return within three days, possibly less, with more troops from the mine." He hesitated, then added, "That is, if the camp officers don't arrest them, and Severus doesn't wipe them out."

"What do you advise, scout?"

Favian said, "I would beg you to return to the valley. Give my men time to join us."

"Our destination is the mines," Helena replied. "And the Lord is my protector."

"My lady, perhaps the Lord has chosen me as his servant."

"Perhaps," Helena conceded. She could sense the others' desire to do as the scout said. Only Macarius remained aloof. He watched swallows soar above the empty fields, still softly humming snatches of the hymn. Helena found herself deeply grateful for their willingness to follow her, even here. No pledge of loyalty, no oath of allegiance could have meant half so much as their patience in the face of such danger.

"We will stay here for the night," she decided. "And I will pray about tomorrow."

: CHAPTER 9 :

:

It was late afternoon by the time they returned to the abandoned farm. Anthony found a lame goat eating green shoots in the neighboring field. He butchered the animal while Cratus started a fire and his men searched the garden for ripe vegetables. They roasted the goat on a spit and spread root vegetables on the hot stones. There was a container of salt in the farm's cookhouse along with a smaller vessel of dried herbs. Macarius made himself useful by turning the spit and ladling the dripping grease onto the roasting vegetables. Anthony helped the guards and Helena's maid erect the little canvas tent. Then they gathered by the fire. Macarius blessed the repast and asked for the scouts' safety. He asked for God's guidance. He asked for mercy and for peace and for healing. They ate together in a companionable silence until Helena asked, "Where are the farmers?"

Anthony had spent the time it had taken to cook their dinner wondering the same thing. "My guess is they're hiding in caves." He pointed to the cliffs lining the southwestern hills. "They'll stock supplies for just such a moment and have one cave blocked off with thorn bushes for the animals."

They all stared toward the setting sun, out where the hills swooped and curved and formed deep shadows. Anthony went on, "There's a small path that runs through the pasture in that direction."

"Could be a game trail," Cratus said.

"Game trails don't have gates," Anthony replied. "There's one at the field's far side."

Helena rose and bid the company goodnight. Anthony stood with the others and saluted the departing figure. If she noticed his gesture, she gave no sign. He volunteered to stand first watch and fed the fire while the others settled on their blankets. He watched the light wane and the first stars emerge. He had always liked such times, when the sky shifted through subtle patterns and his thoughts could roam free.

"May I join you?"

He was twice startled, both because he had heard no footsteps and because the person who addressed him was Helena. "Highness, of course."

Anthony patrolled around the yard's boundary and then halted when they reached the far fence. Helena said, "I heard you speaking with Macarius about your wife and child. I am so sorry for your loss."

"Thank you, my lady."

"Rachel is a Hebrew name."

"My wife was Judean," Anthony confirmed.

"She was a follower of Jesus?"

"She and all her family. Her father was a merchant. Our families traded together." Anthony exhaled a long breath to the silvery sweep of light. "Rachel begged her father to permit us to wed. Her father disliked her marrying a soldier, and a gentile one at that. But he loved his daughter too much to deny her anything."

"And she wanted you," Helena said. "The dashing young officer who had found favor with my son the general."

"All true." He smiled at the memories. "I liked her father. I still do."

"You have seen him since his daughter's passage?"

"Once. The night before I departed to join you."

"You sought him out because you did not expect to return?"

In response, Anthony stared across the fields and gave into the memory. He had knelt before the gray-bearded merchant, weighed down by the sorrow he had seen in the man's eyes. The merchant had said nothing, merely settling his hand upon Anthony's head. They had remained like that for a time, the only sound coming from the sputtering torches and Anthony's horse pawing the ground in the forecourt. But when he had risen, Rachel's father had embraced him, and together they had wept. Those had been the first tears Anthony had shed since laying his wife and child in the earth.

Helena broke into his recollections with, "May I ask why you have not asked about my vision?"

"Cratus told me he follows you out of the respect he holds for you and your son," Anthony replied. "I count that as a good reason to do the same."

"I am grateful for your allegiance, Anthony. It means a very great deal." Helena looked up at the stars. "The night the Lord came to me, he said I was to make this journey, and that I would be safe, and that I was to trust him in all things. He said my travels would become a sign to all the empire."

"A sign of what?"

"I do not know. But at each step of the journey, I have found miracles awaiting me."

Anthony voiced the thought that had perplexed him since his arrival in Cyprus. "I cannot see how your son permitted you to make this journey, much less do so alone."

She nodded slowly. "A miracle, is it not? At first, Constantine refused. Then that night, he heard a voice."

Anthony felt the hairs on his neck rise. "God spoke with your son a second time?"

"And told him that I must make this journey. And do so without an official escort. Because this was a divine mission ordained by God," Helena confirmed. "The next day, he prayed with me and gave me the chest you have helped lash to the donkey's back."

Anthony had seen the two chests, one that opened to reveal more homespun and other personal items. The other had never been opened in his presence before. "Your chest holds money, my lady?"

"Three thousand gold denarii."

Three thousand denarii was enough to buy a palace in Rome and have a lifetime of leisure to enjoy it. Anthony started to complain that such a fortune would attract every bandit in the land but decided such a lure meant nothing beside the threats they already faced.

Helena turned from her inspection of the sky. "What would it take for you to join me on this pilgrimage?"

"I am at your side already."

"You know precisely what I mean."

Anthony hesitated. It seemed to him that the night was listening. And forces gathered beyond the starlit horizon. Not threatening. But attentive. Waiting for his response.

To his surprise, Helena settled her hand upon his arm. Her gaze was filled with dark shadows, and old pain deepened her voice. "You are not the only one who suffers from impossible wounds. I sense in you a kindred spirit, Anthony. And so I extend to you both an invitation and a request. Seek a new purpose for your life, one beyond the reach of your past."

"My lady..."

"Oh, I know what I say sounds impossible. I understand this all too well. Even as I speak, I feel besieged by my past and my failings. I am as weak as you, Anthony. My faith is a fragile thing.

I pray constantly for help and feel as though most of my prayers go unanswered."

Her confession drew him like a beacon aimed at his soul. "What do you want of me?"

"Do as I ask. Join with me in this pilgrimage."

"I am not worthy, my lady."

"Nor am I." Her smile was the saddest he had ever seen. "Please pray on this tonight. Give the Lord a chance to speak to your heart. And I shall pray with you."

* * *

But despite her best intentions, the night proved her a liar. For when Helena awoke, she found herself unable to pray for anyone, even herself. The night besieged her with old ghosts.

The memories savaged her, leaving her feeling as though her tent had become a canvas prison. She clawed away the coverlet and rose from her bedding. She entered the starlight and turned away from the sentry. She wanted to speak with no one. She wanted solitude. She wanted air. She wanted...

The images chased her across the farmyard, over to where the scarred fence bordered the empty corral. If she had known her confession to Anthony would have released her memories, she would never have opened her mouth. Helena clenched the rough wood and fought to reseal the secret door. But the images whispered and danced and shredded her heart.

Helena had spent years awaiting the day when her general would come home—the dashing young officer she had wed, grown old and matured, finally ready to hang up his sword. Ready to withdraw from the rule of force and from armies and from combat. Ready to join her in their seaside villa. Ready to tend his vineyards. Ready to be content. With her. Together.

She had sought to make a home where her husband and their son would find a cherished haven. A place where they all could smile and laugh and love. That was all Helena had wanted for her autumn years. The wonderful times of her early marriage ripened in the fullness of years. Their marriage and their lives enriched and deepened and...

Helena lifted her face to the night. The stars were a silver sheen beyond her veil of tears. Her silent cry stretched her neck so taut her shoulders ached. She begged God to remove this dagger from her heart. She begged for healing and for peace. She did not miss her husband. She missed what might have been. She knew it was probably wrong, that she was indulging in old regrets. But telling herself this did not remove the piercing ache to her heart or lift the weight from her. She implored and she wept and she pleaded. Just as she had done so many times before. And, as always, God remained silent.

When she finally regained control, she turned and started back to her tent.

Then she saw them.

Three sets of eyes watched her.

Anthony and Cratus stood by their bedrolls. The other guards and the scout slumbered at their feet. Macarius stood on the fire's other side, leaning heavily upon his cane. The three of them respected her solitude. They did not speak, nor did they approach. They shared the same expression, soldiers and bishop alike. They were solemn and grave and alert. Their gazes said it all. They were there to serve her. There to offer strength. There to struggle with her against the night.

Helena reentered her tent. As she lay back down beside her slumbering maid, she decided that God had indeed answered her prayer after all.

: CHAPTER 10 :

:

The next morning, Helena approached the scouts officer and agreed to wait one more day, so that his men could arrive and themselves have a night's rest. Anthony and the other guards breathed easier, released from a tension they had half-hidden until it was gone.

Macarius led a prayer after breakfast. Anthony stood apart from the others and watched the priest become illuminated with the joy of speaking to his Lord. Anthony recalled how his wife had been like that. Rachel had never been more alive than when praying. The service ended, and Constantine's mother gestured for him to join her inside her tent. Anthony moved toward the tent, hollowed by how Rachel's faith had not been enough to keep their marriage or their son alive.

Helena greeted him with, "Have you thought upon our discussion?"

"I have, my lady."

"Have you prayed about it?"

Anthony could find no evidence of the anguish Helena had revealed while praying to the moonlit night. Yet, he felt as though her most vulnerable moment granted the ability to confess. "I have not spoken with God since the day I laid my son and wife in the earth."

Helena seemed pleased by his response. Which surprised him. Most spiritual folk took his weakness of faith as a personal insult.

Instead, Helena said, "You are an honest man, even when most would find a reason to lie. You are straight and true when a deviation from course would be safer." She settled into the camp-chair, a folding stool with arms. "I like you, Centurion. I am glad you are here."

Anthony found himself thinking how much the mother was like the son, sparse in motion, piercing in wisdom. "What's the point?"

"I beg your pardon?"

"Become a pilgrim. Give feet to prayer. Beseech God...for what?"

To his surprise, he heard Macarius say, "My lady, might I be permitted to join you?"

"Please do," Helena agreed.

Macarius pushed through the tent flap and limped over to stand beside Helena. "Makes for a change, hearing someone speak the truth about their doubts. The first step of becoming a pilgrim is accepting that your life is not perfect."

"I have no problem there," Anthony replied.

"You must acknowledge a need that you cannot resolve yourself," Macarius went on.

"You seek what you do not have," Helena said, her voice carrying the gravity of one who spoke from experience. "And what you seek contains a spiritual element."

"This is the key," Macarius agreed. "Too often we see the absence of peace or calm or hope or health as belonging only to this world. And yet so often the problem we face is only the barest edge. Buried deep within us is a greater need. One that is directly linked to our spiritual life. It is for this reason that we take the pilgrim's road."

The shadows aged Helena far beyond her years. "We are dragged down by the unfairness of life. We are burdened by pains we do not deserve. I have come to Judea because my God called me. But I have my own reasons as well, my own needs, my own hopes for a better tomorrow. And I know that the answer to this personal plea can only come through a closer walk with our Lord."

Anthony was surprised to find the answer there before him. His burning need formed a cauldron that forced out the words, "Make me want to live again. That is the sign I ask for."

Helena studied him intently, but it was Macarius who said, "You are asking to be granted a new purpose for your life."

"Aye. I suppose I am."

The bishop smiled. "But how is God to redirect your mind and heart if you do not ask him?"

Anthony did not know how to respond. When he remained silent, Helena said, "On the day this happens, you agree to join me upon the pilgrim road?"

"I will, my lady."

"For now, this will do." Helena pulled parchment and pen and ink from her portable table. Anthony assumed it was so as to write out his promise. It was a Roman custom to seal any verbal agreement with a document where both parties set their seal. Instead, Helena said, "My son has granted me the powers to enlist whom I wish and appoint them to whatever post I choose. I want you promoted to a position that gives you authority over everyone who joins us. I am therefore appointing you tribune. Macarius, you will witness this act?"

"It will be my honor, my lady."

Anthony was struck speechless. A tribune was second in command to the legion's senior general. The full title was *tribunus laticlavius*, and the appointment was normally given to a man expected to rise from the military into politics. The tribune served as the personal representative of the Roman emperor. Anthony watched as Helena finished writing and offered the pen to Macarius, who witnessed the edict. She accepted the royal seal from her maid and applied it to wax she melted with her candle.

When Helena sealed the parchment and handed it to him, all Anthony could manage was a very weak, "Thank you, my lady."

Helena rose and stepped to the chest that resided by her sleeping pallet. She used a key suspended from a chain on her wrist to unlock it. "I am also assigning you responsibility for our funds."

Anthony accepted a roll bound in a thin strip of cedar and sealed with red wax. He broke the seal and watched as the heavy gold coins spilled into his hands.

Helena relocked the chest. "I want you to find the farmers. Pay them for the use of their farm and the animal."

"My lady, one of these could buy the entire farm and those to either side."

"I am well aware of that. See if there are Christians among them. If so, tell them to use the remainder of this money to rebuild their church."

He could think of nothing to say, so he bowed and retreated into the sunlight.

Anthony crossed the farmyard and went through the rear gate. As he followed the faint trail, he found himself sorely tempted to be happy. Which was dangerous. It invited him to want a future. It lured him to hope they might survive.

* * *

The farmers were where Anthony expected to find them. The cave dwellings were situated in a natural curve of the cliffside, hiding them from the road. Anthony heard a child singing, but the sound was stifled as he rounded the stone headland. He planted his sword in the earth and approached unarmed.

But the farmers had learned to fear all Romans, armed or not. They sent one wizened elder out alone. Anthony saluted the old man but then regretted the gesture. "Do any of your folk follow Jesus?"

The elder's knees almost buckled in fear. "W-What?"

Anthony drew the dirk from his belt. The old man groaned in rising terror. Anthony squatted and drew a fish in the dirt between them. The sign had become a universal symbol in such dangerous times, easily erased or redrawn into the symbol for one of the temple sects.

He stood and asked again, "Are there followers among you?"

The man gave a tremulous nod. "We all are, sir."

"What, the entire valley?"

"Here and beyond. Brought to faith by Peter himself. My grandfather told me of that day. As did his grandfather before him."

"Yet you have no church."

"Gone, good sir. Gone these last many years. We burned it to the ground. To save our young ones."

"You still teach your children the Way?"

The elder gestured to the caves behind him. A number of fearful faces had emerged from the shadows to observe the exchange. "Our hideaway serves well enough for that. The young ones all learn the letters and the holy text. You can see their scribblings on the wall if you have a desire."

Anthony shook his head to the invitation. "You have heard of Helena?"

"No, sir. I can't say that I have."

"She is mother of Constantine, general of the northern armies. Remember those names." Anthony held out two gold denarii. "This is for you. Take honest payment for the farm where we camped and for what we ate. Use the rest to rebuild your church."

The old man's eyes widened at the sight of so much wealth. He made no move to accept the gift. "It isn't safe."

"A new law rules the land. You will no longer be scourged for your faith." Anthony reached forward and forced the coins into his hand. "Take this as proof. And go with God."

Where the trail met the headland, Anthony glanced back. The old man still stood watching him, his face glistening in the rising sun.

: CHAPTER 11 :

:

Early that afternoon, Favian's scouts trudged into camp. They did not actually tiptoe around Helena. They were far too tired for any such behavior. But that was how it felt to her. As though they treaded lightly about the dust, like some of the courtiers she had seen on her visits to Rome. Afraid they might break the mood or disturb the air. She welcomed them solemnly, and they responded with the same grief-stricken shame as Evander. She accepted their apology and their guilt and felt like a liar as she did so.

It seemed to Helena that the day held its breath. The empty fields only added to the sense of expectancy. The newly arrived scouts ate a meal prepared from supplies they had brought on their own backs and then collapsed exhausted in the shade and slept. Cratus, her stalwart guard, sat on a corner of the watering trough and alternated between studying the looming hills and searching the fields for Anthony's return. As he did, he sharpened his sword. The sound of the whetstone sliding along the blade counted down the minutes. They would leave with the dawn. The hills awaited. Helena did her best not to look in that direction.

She knew these were probably her last safe hours. Perhaps even the final full day she would draw breath. She knew she should be grateful for the newly arrived guards and the devotion they already offered her. She knew she should rest. Pray. Prepare. But as the afternoon dragged and Anthony did not appear, her thoughts returned time and again to the previous night and how the memories had assaulted her. Finally, she sought out Macarius. Helena walked with him to the distant fence, waved her maid back to the camp, and said, "I feel as though I am under attack."

"That is hardly a surprise, my lady."

"I'm not worried about death. Not my own, at least. Risking the lives of others troubles me terribly. If I could, I would order them to abandon me."

"What if the scouts officer is correct, and he serves here at God's command?" When her only response was to begin pacing the furrowed earth before him, he went on, "I urge you not to say anything. They won't agree, and it would only lead to dissent in an hour when peace and harmony are needed."

"But I have none of my own!" The words were a scalding rush. "I feel anything *but* peace! My mind has become my enemy! My husband prowls my nights! I can't rise above past pains. I can't forget. I can't forgive. I can't see my way out of this. I can't focus on God. I can't..."

"You can do nothing," Macarius supplied. "You are powerless. Helpless. Without God's help..."

His quiet understanding released the unwanted tears. "I am failing my Lord."

"You are doing anything but."

"I feel like such a fraud. I speak with Anthony and offer him such confident words. Then the next moment I feel weak and frail and lost."

"You are human."

"I have been given a vision. I have heard the Lord's voice. I need to rise above all these chains that hold me down."

"If you had the strength to do this, what would be your need of him? If you had a constant peace all your own, why should you draw closer to God?"

Helena stopped and looked at him. Macarius held the staff in one hand and with the other supported himself on the corral fence. It seemed to Helena that a smile lurked just beneath his scarred visage.

Macarius went on, "When did our Lord come to you? In your hour of desolation, yes? As he did with David and Moses and Ezekiel. When your strength was gone and hope lost, what did he say?" Macarius stabbed the earth with his staff. "*I* am your strength. Put your faith in *me*."

"Why doesn't he say these things to me now, when I need him most?"

"Because he wants you human. He wants you to be as the others are with whom you will meet and share and toil and weep. He wants you to know their suffering, and live it, and be his beacon."

* * *

When Anthony returned to the farmyard camp, he reported that the farmers had accepted the money and agreed to rebuild their church. He met Favian's band of scouts. He ate a meal. Then they gathered for an evening Eucharist. Anthony joined the others. He accepted the cup and the bread from the scarred priest. He saw how the scouts wept with gratitude and grief when it came their turn. Afterward, he stretched out on his bedroll, grateful that for this one night he could sleep without standing watch, for the scouts had rested all day and were eager to share the duties. He lay and observed as sparks rose from the fire and joined the stars overhead. In the distance, the hills loomed. Waiting.

The next morning, they set off.

As they trudged along the road, Favian walked up alongside him and demanded, "The lady intends to go on foot?"

"All the way to Jerusalem. As I told you yesterday. She journeys as a pilgrim."

The scouts officer led his mount by the reins. He patted his horse's flank, using the gesture to glance back at where Helena walked alongside the priest's donkey. "What is she like?"

"I have only known her a few days. I was sent by Constantine with a message and joined them in Cyprus." Anthony had no idea how to describe the way Helena unsettled him. How she seemed an impossible combination. How she was both aloof and caring, distant and intensely connected, divinely inspired and very human, strong and frail at the same time. He changed the subject with, "How far to the mine?"

"With a good horse and safe passage, you could push through one long day and arrive by nightfall. On foot, holding to a woman's pace..." He squinted at the sunlit road ahead. "Three days?"

"Is there a place where we can stop for the night?"

"We should reach the highland valley's one oasis by late afternoon." Favian grimaced. "I doubt we will find safety there."

"I suggest you scout the road ahead. Split your other men into two bands to walk before and behind us." But as Favian started to climb into the saddle, Anthony motioned for him to remain where he was. "The lady has appointed me tribune."

The scouts officer could have responded any number of ways. How such an appointment, done by a general's mother far from the army he commanded, held less weight than the parchment in Anthony's pouch. Or that a scouts officer from one of Rome's high families could scarcely be expected to stand duty under such a flimsy excuse of an appointment.

Instead, Favian demanded, "All who join will be followers of Jesus?"

"That is my hope and my intention," Anthony replied. He started to add, "If we survive long enough to bring the troops together." But he held back.

Favian declared, "I and my men are yours to command."

Anthony gave that a moment's silent gratitude and then said, "We will hold a swearing-in...When the proper moment arises."

Favian understood him well enough. He glanced at the hills and said grimly, "All that is in God's hands."

* * *

The road swept in broad curves around a series of pinnacles, climbing steadily. They entered a shallow vale rimmed on all sides by razor-edged hills. The road ran straight and true down the valley's heart. There was not a breath of wind.

By early afternoon, they tromped through an oven. The air carried the pungent odor of wild sorrel. The sweat dried as fast as Anthony's body poured it out. Favian's men kept position a hundred paces before and behind them. Favian trotted in a steady circle, his horse walking with head lowered and bridle dripping foam.

Then the trumpet sounded.

The call was jarring in the still air, clear and precise as a well-aimed blade. The entire group halted. The men drew their swords, a great clattering of weapons. Anthony spotted the man first. "To your right, on the ridgeline."

The man was too far away for his features to be clear. But the burnished gold of his breastplate shone like a beacon of doom. Favian wheeled his weary mount and gave chase. The assassin observed their approach in utter stillness. He only turned his horse away when the scouts officer started to climb the hill. As Severus cantered from the ridge, he lifted his curved horn in a mock salute.

When Favian returned, he declared to Helena, "Mistress, you must ride or perish."

Helena did not even acknowledge he had spoken. The woman had trudged all day, and though her step was slower, she did not falter.

Favian sawed the reins and led his weary mount back to where Anthony walked as rear guard. "Can you not make her listen? If the attack comes, it would be aimed at her. Her life could well depend upon a swift escape."

Anthony stared at the woman in gray. Her robe was stained white with salt from her perspiration. Yet her stance was regal. "She would never leave us."

Favian started to respond but thought better of it and spurred his horse on ahead.

Another hour passed. Sunlight danced and shimmered. The high desert appeared to be on fire, weaving and shivering through the sweat that almost blinded Anthony.

And in that moment, his Rachel came to him.

Anthony knew it was a mirage. And yet he was helpless to do anything about it. His breath rasped in his own ears. The road was nothing save a molten ribbon. The only thing he could see clearly was a woman who had been in her grave for almost a year.

During her pregnancy, Rachel had taken to sitting in the sunlight like a contented cat. The closer she drew to birthing their first child, the harder it became for her to feel warm. She sat with eyes closed and stroked her belly. Anthony often slipped up beside her, content to sit in their small garden and observe the joy that bathed her features. He had never dreamed such happiness could be his.

Anthony swiped at his eyes, the motion returning him to this moment, robbing him of any desire for another day, another breath. All lost.

Another dozen steps and a different memory came to him, as fierce and powerful as the blinding sunlight. He had forgotten it until that instant. But now, it was far more clear than the highland valley through which he trekked.

The dawn of her final day on earth, he had awoken to find Rachel seated in the chair by their bed, staring at him. Their customary places had been reversed, with he the one resting and she the one watching.

When she saw that he was awake, Rachel told him, "You will do great things."

He had struggled to rub away the sleep. "What?"

"God has whispered your name. He has called you to rise up. Beyond where you are."

"All I want is to love you and our child," he replied, feeling as though the words rose from his overfull heart.

"You must be willing to grow," she replied softly. "You must become his servant."

"I serve Constantine," Anthony replied. "That is enough for any man."

"You will do both. And more. Through your hands, miracles will take form. If you accept."

She went silent. He swung his feet to the floor and reached for her hand. "Accept what?"

She kissed his face. "You must ask that of God, not me."

It was only now, as he trudged the final mile to the oasis, that Anthony realized he had never done as his wife had asked. As the first green tips of the trees appeared in the hazy distance, he feared he had left her final bequest until far too late.

CHAPTER 12

Two hours later, the bleak desert became blanketed by waist-high grass. The dry season was upon them, and the brittle stalks rustled feverishly in the hot wind. The sound mocked Helena's determination to force her exhausted body onward. Then, just as she was ready to admit defeat, Helena spied a distant ring of palms.

Her rigid determination faltered, and she gripped the bishop's donkey to keep herself upright. Everyone's attention became captured by the prospect of shade and rest and water. Together they hurried onward.

A small pool was fed from an underground spring. A dry creek bed meandered down from the closest hills, and along its path, the grass grew thicker still. Date palms bordered the pool, and quail fluttered about, picking seeds from the high grass. Helena settled on a stone by the pond and dipped a cloth into the cool water. She bathed her face and reveled in the sensation that the day's trek was finally at an end. She struggled to focus her tired mind on the thought that had whispered to her just as she had left the road. There, in the shimmering waters, she saw it clearly.

She had to forgive herself.

On one level, it was ludicrous. What had she done to deserve her fate? She had every right to be hurt, wounded, angry, and even to seek vengeance.

On the other, she knew the truth of this matter. She did not need anyone to be hard on her. She was harder on herself than anyone else could possibly be. Nothing she did was ever good enough. She had spent an entire lifetime striving to do better, to rise further, to be more. Which, of course, was one reason why she remained so upset with her husband. Because he had both failed to live up to her expectations and dragged her down as well.

Favian directed two of his men to rig snares to catch their dinner while Cratus and another guard set up Helena's tent. Anthony ordered the footsore scouts to rest and eat and prepare for the long night ahead. He and Favian then returned to the road and walked on ahead.

Helena sat apart and argued with herself. Personal forgiveness meant accepting that she was flawed. Imperfect. Destined to miss the mark, time and again. She doubted whether she was able to actually, honestly, take that step.

* * *

Anthony and Favian scaled a lone mound that rose to the right of the road between their camp and the ridge they would climb the next day, if they survived the night. It was not much of a hill, scarcely the height of ten men and shaped like an upended bowl. But from its top Anthony could see the entire valley.

From that perspective, their oasis camp was an open invitation to every bandit on earth—a single tent, a cluster of men, an exhausted horse. Smoke from their lone campfire rose like a beacon.

"We could move the camp up here," Favian suggested doubtfully.

Anthony shook his head. "This slope is so gentle a baby could scale it."

"Perhaps a lookout?"

It was tempting, but Anthony decided, "Our numbers are already too small. Besides, we know Severus is there. We know they are coming."

Then he sensed a change. He turned around, tasting the air. The grass began where the creek bed emerged from the hills and extended out like a silver-gray carpet, rustling and nervous. It ended two hundred paces beyond the oasis, probably where the water reached during the wet season. Anthony looked back at the camp. The campfire's smoke began drifting toward the cliffs. Then he felt it again, a subtle shift to the breeze, scarcely more than a breath, yet enough to rattle the dry leaves. When it happened a third time, he turned so as to face directly into the shifting wind. Gradually, the wind strengthened, blowing straight along the direction from which they had come. He asked, "Where would you attack from?"

Favian's answer was immediate. He pointed to a gorge that cleaved a shadowy hollow into the ridgeline. "I'd already have my troops waiting in that defile. Then I'd send a few horsemen across the valley floor from the other direction to draw our attention and harry us."

It was precisely what Anthony had been thinking. The gorge was so deep that he suspected the creek had been a raging river eons earlier. Above the shadows rose a vertical ledge, still polished by a waterfall that had not run for centuries. "Back to camp."

The wind strengthened as the sun dipped below the stone-rimmed horizon. The peaks shone like beaten gold, a desert symphony of silent glory. They gathered for a final prayer and the sacraments. The light went ruddy, then rust, and faded to where the night could sweep forward and blanket them with stars. Anthony watched as Macarius spoke, but all he could hear was the echo of his wife's final challenge.

They sat by the campfire and ate a fine meal of roast quail spiced with sorrel, flatbread, dates and all the tea they could drink. The soldiers ate like soldiers everywhere, storing up for the long night ahead. Anthony saw no need to save food for a morning they might well not live to greet.

The moon rose above the far ridge, transforming the waist-high grass into a silver sea that sighed and rushed in the strengthening wind. Overhead, the palm fronds rattled excitedly, as though doing their best to warn Anthony and the others of unseen foes.

Anthony chose five men, Favian among them, and strung them out between the camp and the gorge. Each man tended a small fire. The rest he set under Cratus, to rim the camp with spear and sword and shield. Favian's horse he tethered inside the camp, there for a last minute flight. If there was time, he was determined to save the empress.

When he had done all he could, Anthony walked away from camp and crouched at the rim of the rustling grass. Ahead of him was a moonlit expanse of dry and empty desert. In the far distance rose the valley's rim, a ragged silhouette carved from the night.

The day's heat was gone now. The night wind carried a chilling edge. Anthony draped a blanket around his shoulders and tried to tell himself the faint stirrings in his gut were merely a soldier's instincts to fight and survive to fight again. But the high desert night was too clear for such lies. He sensed the return of his late wife's final words and felt them plant new seeds in his heart. They sprouted with a fierce determination, creating a rising clamor that filled his being. Over and over, four words rose within him. *I want to live!*

He knelt there on the dry earth and bowed his head. As he did so, it seemed that the surrounding rustle became transformed into the hushed whisper of a thousand voices, all joined with him in a prayer it had taken a lifetime to speak. "Lord, if I am to die, let it be to your glory. If I am to live, let it be in your service. Whatever comes, help me to meet it according to your will. Amen."

As he lifted his head, he was certain Rachel had joined him. There in the dry chill wind and the whispering grass, he sensed that he had come very close indeed to heaven.

CHAPTER 13

As he started back to camp, Anthony heard the plaintive call of a night bird. It was far in the distance, almost lost in the wind. Anthony spotted a flickering light on the high ridge above the gorge. The signal fire dipped once and then vanished. As he raced back to camp, he heard Cratus bark, the old soldier calling his troops to full alert.

Out of the empty desert reaches, they came. The drumming horses raced along the road, silhouetted against the moonlight. Almost as though they wanted to be seen and draw the camp's attention away from a larger threat that sneaked through the grass behind them. Anthony had staked their lives on this expectation.

He bounded back into camp, yelling, "They come! They come! Favian!"

From the rustling distance, there came a response, "Here!"

"Fire the grass!"

Anthony did not wait for a response. He trusted the scouts officer to do his job. He gathered his tiny force and turned to face the incoming foe.

Down from the road, the nine horsemen thundered. They raced through the grass, aiming straight for the oasis. Firelight glinted off curved Parthian blades and turbans laced with gold thread. At their fore rode Severus.

The attackers shrieked their blood lust as they circled the pond and made for them. They made a great spectacle of their attack, waving their great blades overhead and making so as to plunge straight into their flimsy line.

"Hold fast!" Anthony had no shield but stood between two of the scouts who did. He planted his spear in the dirt. Others did likewise, forming a deadly barrier of steel. At the last minute, Severus and his warriors wheeled to the left and raced past.

Cratus shouted, "They're preparing for another attack!"

"Hold steady!" Anthony called in reply.

Then they heard the flames.

The fire rose in a glorious rout, a virtual explosion of light and sparks. The Judean dry season was coming to an end, and according to Favian, it had not rained for three long months. The highland grass stood parched and ready to ignite. If anything, the wind strengthened as Favian lit the fireline. The sound was a hungry roar, and somewhere in the distance rose an answering shriek. The sound was so piercing it halted the horsemen in their tracks. Then another cry arose, then any number of voices shouting and calling.

"Hold fast!" Anthony watched the mounted attackers and knew this was the most dangerous moment, as a desire for vengeance might cause them to launch a suicide assault. "Eyes front!"

Then Severus shouted to his men in an unknown tongue. The attackers snarled at Anthony before wheeling about and disappearing. Severus was the last to depart. His smile carried a deadly light; his voice carried over the fire's roar. "We will meet again. Of that you can be assured."

Severus raced away. The hooves drummed hard upon the earth, grew dimmer, and then were swallowed by the night.

Favian and his men came leaping out of the darkness, all of them blackened by ash. "Are they gone?"

"For the moment. Helena? Macarius?"

"We are well." The woman sounded impossibly calm. "Is it over?"

"Not yet, my lady." He motioned for Favian and his crew to join their line. "Stay alert."

Too soon the flames died. The conflagration climbed partway up the ridgeline, to where the grasses stopped growing. They watched the fire split into tiny glowing segments and then die away altogether.

Anthony searched the distance. In the moonlight, he saw nine horsemen emerge from the blackened field, Severus at their lead. They were joined by eight more riders, and they by men on foot, until Anthony and his meager band faced a force too numerous to count. The marauders started for them with blades glinting.

Severus called out, "Savor the night! The wind! Even the ash, does it not call to you? Soon you will feel the flames of your own pyre, the ash of your own doom!"

Cratus muttered, "No Roman officer would waste his breath in such a manner."

"Severus takes pleasure in the terror of his foes," Favian replied. "Don't let them take you alive."

But before Anthony could repeat his command to stand ready, he heard a different sound. A trumpet's clarion call rose from the road ahead.

The sound was so unexpected as to confuse them all. Then it blew again, calling Roman legionnaires to arms. In response, voices rose in unison, shouting the battle cry, taking the fight to the enemy.

Roman horsemen streamed off the road, a veritable flood of fighting men, pouring into the enemy's flank.

They were saved.

CHAPTER 14

A̲n hour after dawn, Helena and the others rejoined the road. As she started another day's trek, she reflected how there was nothing that focused the mind like facing the final breath.

They were all exhausted by the attack and the lack of decent rest. Even so, none of them wished to remain at the oasis an instant longer. The field to their right was now a vast plain of smoldering rubble. Thankfully, the mild morning breeze blew away from them. Ash streaked the distant hills, as though writing the tale of their survival in a dark desert script.

Helena walked as usual alongside Macarius and his donkey. Now and then, she reached out and stroked the beast's flank. What she wanted, however, was to hold the bishop's hand. He had held it the previous night, the first time she had touched him for more than the instant required to accept the Eucharist offering. She glanced over. Macarius gazed away from her, over the burnt field to the gorge that cleaved a great fissure into the ridge. The bishop was as ugly a figure as she had ever known. His face looked ravaged. His wrinkles were so deep they might as well have been scored by a blade. His jaw bore two days of stubble. Now and then, his shoulders jerked, as though he suffered from palsy. His hands were bent and arthritic. His robe was streaked with ash and sweat. His sandals were old and torn and poorly repaired. His only adornment was a simple wooden cross, suspended around his neck by a strip of uncured leather.

He also possessed, Helena decided, the most engaging smile she had ever seen.

"Today is a day of making big decisions," she declared. "Decisions that lead to change."

Macarius studied the line of weary soldiers ahead of them. The soldiers numbered forty-seven now. Evander rode horses from the mine's stables, as did about half of the three dozen men who had returned with him. Anthony had split the men into three groups. Outriders patrolled the distance, while others guarded the way ahead and the road behind. "Anthony tells me that all these soldiers have asked to serve under him."

"Did you not hear what I said?"

"Indeed I did, my lady. It was a grand idea, appointing him tribune. Of course, when word of your action reaches Damascus, Maximinus will be furious." The thought clearly delighted Macarius. "Your son would be so proud of you."

"You do not even know Constantine."

"But I am coming to know you, my lady." As he smiled, the scars and furrows rearranged themselves, accenting his joy. "And through you, an image of your son is taking shape."

"I have known many compliments in my time, but that perhaps is the finest."

He bowed from the horse's back. "You were speaking of decisions."

"I was indeed." Her limbs felt leaden. They had many hot and exhausting miles to cover and another steep climb to make out of the highland valley. And yet she felt almost giddy with relief. She recalled the hour of the attack, and the screams, and the feel of death approaching from all sides. "Last night I thought we were finished."

"It was a close-run thing," Macarius agreed.

"You did not appear the least bit frightened, kneeling with me there in the tent."

"I have faced death more times than I care to count. And each time, I am terrified. Last night was no different." He flicked the reins, brushing a fly from the donkey's ear. "You spoke of—"

"Decisions. Yes. I want to stop feeling so trapped by my past. I want to grow beyond where I am. I want to be, well, better."

"A wise and worthy destination."

"Last night was a gift. Today is a gift. I want to use them wisely." She hesitated and then confessed, "I feel that God is calling me to forgive myself."

She expected many things. A gentle suggestion, perhaps, that she redirect her efforts to a more worthy goal. Anything but what happened, which was that Macarius lifted his head to the sky and laughed out loud. The sound was so unexpected it halted the guards on flank. Faces all about them turned and stared. If Macarius noticed at all, he gave no sign. "A challenge worthy of the woman you are."

"You are not laughing at me?"

"My lady, I laugh in admiration. There is no quest I would find harder. I am laughing with relief, because God has leveled the challenge at you and not me." He rubbed a scraggly cheek. "Though it occurs to me that I should heed the call as well. Which fills me with genuine dread."

She thought of the bishop's family and the man who had wielded the knife. Severus had not been seen that morning. But she could sense his presence. She could almost smell the assassin. "You are a good man, Macarius. I am glad you are with us."

He bowed in his saddle. "It is an honor to serve the mistress called to God's quest."

"You have never asked what that quest might be," she pointed out. "Or what the vision revealed."

"I have started to," Macarius confessed. "Last night, before the attack. I wanted to know why we were here, in case..."

She nodded. Understanding.

"Then I decided it was an act of weakness, confessing to a curiosity out of fear. So I remained silent."

"I do not know why I hold back," she confessed. "Only that the time does not seem right."

"So you should wait," the bishop said decisively. "And I will wait with you."

She grew silent, as the climb up the ridgeline road claimed her every vestige of strength and breath. The plains were empty now. The only indication of the night's struggle was the ash blanketing the earth from the pool to the gorge. One lonely hill rose from the black earth, its windward side etched with veins of cinders. They were all weary, none more than Helena, but no one suggested they make camp. Helena and Macarius traveled apart from the others. She could sense their desire to treat her with deference, and this isolation was the result. She knew even if she asked them to join her, the seclusion would remain. She felt the loneliness of her life sweep over her. Then with a weary swipe of her hand, she waved it aside.

She asked Macarius, "Have you ever experienced a vision?"

"If you mean, has God spoken to me or shown me images of the beyond, no. If you mean, has God shown me the impossible gift of peace when all the world has told me to despair," he stopped and smiled at the road ahead. "Then yes. I have known the glory of God."

She followed the direction of his gaze. The road baked yellow and shimmering beneath the Judean sun. For once, it beckoned to her. "I know there are dangers ahead. I know we are chased by a trained killer. I know I have a world of reasons to worry. I know I am frail. What I *want* is to look beyond all that."

Slowly, Macarius turned back. His good eye gleamed as he observed her in silence.

"I want to be ready to serve at God's command. And I can't do this if I let fear and regret and anger dominate my life. I want to turn from all that. I want to focus on God. But I don't know if I can."

Macarius took her hand as he had the previous night. "Let us pray on this. And keep praying. And trust God both to answer and to give you the strength to hear."

: CHAPTER 15 :

:

At dusk, they made camp by a village's lone well. Makeshift stands offered hearty fare—flatbread and lamb and new season grapes and olives and cheese. When they finished eating, Helena knelt for the evening prayers and then entered her tent, eased into her bedroll, and knew nothing more until dawn.

At sunrise, she watched as the men gathered in ranks before Anthony. Evander and Favian and Cratus stood at their fore, and together they all swore fealty to the new Judean cohort. Forty-seven soldiers did not make up a troop, much less form the basis for a new army. Even so, Helena still found it a moving occasion.

Anthony then addressed them, "We are here to serve and protect the general's mother. By serving Helena, we serve Constantine, the first general in Rome's history to follow the Risen One. Constantine does not command his troops to be believers, for he considers a man's faith to be a matter of conscience. In this too, he forges a new path. But Constantine welcomes all followers of Jesus, as do I."

Anthony took a step back, turned smartly, and faced Helena. He nodded to Evander, who barked, "Troop, attention!" When the feet stamped into position, he called out the new salutation Anthony had decided upon, "Helena and Jerusalem!"

It seemed to Helena that more than fifty-odd voices shouted it back. Perhaps it was the warm air, or the words echoing off the ridge they had just climbed. Or perhaps, just perhaps, unseen others found reason to add their voices to the call.

After the swearing-in, Helena joined them for prayer and the sacraments. The new arrivals crowded in close to observe an empress take the cup and the bread from one of their own and hand it to another. Such a thing had never happened in all their lives. Many faces were awash in tears before the ceremony ended.

They walked all day. Anthony's aim was to camp that night in the village that served the mine. Helena continued along the road, guarded by forty-seven men drawn from half a dozen legions. She knew all her men had disgraced themselves by publicly turning from their faith. She knew they remained scarred by more than battle. Together they headed south because that was the route she had chosen for them. They did so in silent trust. They had sworn allegiance, though they did not know the purpose behind their trek.

She had become accustomed to the realms of power, where allowing someone to become close meant risking a request for something that she might have to deny. Once an appeal was turned down, they became enemies. Allies, on the other hand, understood the need for distance. It had been a long time since Helena had been comfortable using the word *friend*.

And yet this was the only word that described how she felt about these men. Cast out by their society, scorned for their beliefs, considered of no more worth than the most brutal prison guard. Her friends.

They halted at midday by a grove of desert pine. There was no well, but the horses had been fed and watered before setting off that morning, and they all carried water skins. A soft breeze came off the sea, which remained hidden beyond soft rolling hills. The air was cool for a change, and the smell of salt very strong. Most of the men sat where they could see the dust-cloud that loomed in the south. Helena knew the yellow haze marked the mine called Phaneao and that for many of her troops it hung like a banner over the worst and most shameful of their deeds. For her, it only added impetus to her need to move beyond her own limitations. Helena found a pair of pines whose trunks grew into a comfortable support and blocked her view of the southern road. She ate her meal and reflected that if she could not make these changes for herself, she could at least strive to become the leader these men deserved.

Midway through her repast, she heard a horse and knew it meant one of the scouts was returning. She did not bother to turn around. She heard Favian report, "The road ahead is clear."

Anthony demanded, "Any sign of Severus?"

"We caught sight of several Parthians. But they remained atop distant hills. We are being tracked, that much I can confirm. Whether or not Severus is among them, I have no idea."

Favian was quiet a long moment before asking, "Does the empress understand what lies ahead?"

Helena started to reveal herself to the men, but before she could rise, she heard Anthony reply, "Helena is mother of one general and the ex-wife of another. She has seen battle. She knows what a Roman mine entails."

"Does she know Phaneao was created just to hold Christians? Does she know when the ranks were filled to bursting, the governor in Damascus ordered the camp commandant to mine salt from the sea?" Favian's voice turned raw from the effort of speaking. "Does Helena know he also ordered us, his sworn troops, to hasten the prisoners' deaths?"

Anthony's voice carried the concern that Helena felt rising in her own heart. "When Helena landed at Caesarea, her first deed was to visit the arena. She asked the jailer where the Christians were imprisoned."

"Why?"

"She has not said. But this is what I suspect: By now, the governor of Damascus will have received word from his consul that Helena is here. The governor will have read his copy of the Edict of Milan. And what will the governor do?" When Favian's only response was to struggle anew for breath, Anthony finished, "He will order all the prisoners killed and their remains hidden. He will deny all his actions. He may even do away with the soldiers who guarded the mine, so that no witness survives to testify against him."

"So Helena…"

"Helena goes to do God's will."

CHAPTER 16

As they gathered for prayer and then broke camp the next day, the men grew increasingly somber. Helena knew it was because of what lay ahead. The yellow cloud loomed heavy, dominating the horizon. Even so, she remained untouched either by their destination or the men's uncertain gloom. Her mind remained held by something that had come to her during the prayer service. It had been more than a memory and less than a vision. Instead, it felt as though she had been whispered a message by a friend. She could almost hear the voice, though nothing had been said. It was all so strangely beautiful that she could walk toward the ominous yellow wall and remain untouched.

She recalled her final night in her father's inn. He had been an official of the local region, like his father before him. The Romans had granted her father the title of king, a mocking salute to how he had surrendered on the eve of war. The members of Helena's clan were fishermen and farmers, a hardy folk who seldom traveled and sought no honor in battle. Some had called her father a traitor, but such talk soon died, as word arrived of other clans being wiped out, whole communities destroyed. In return for bringing peace, the Romans allowed Helena's father to establish an inn used by soldiers and locals alike. Her family was the first of their clan to know Jesus as Lord, offered by a wandering Frank, a man who called himself a priest without a church. Helena recalled how the priest's voice and eyes had burned with a holy fire as he spoke of the Risen One. As the road snaked over a final crest, she whispered to both her father's memory and to the Father of all, "I want to make you proud."

Then they climbed the final rise, and the mine came into view.

* * *

The open pit was shaped like a half-bowl and faced the sea. It was carved into a series of huge steps, like a macabre theater. Far below them, down where the stage would have been, stretched a blindingly white field. It extended from one side of the pit to the other, perhaps a mile and a half in width, and was separated into regular squares. The drying salt reflected the sunlight with glittering intensity.

Beyond the salt farm, a pair of ships were anchored to the shore, waiting to be loaded with supplies.

Two rope pulley systems climbed the pit's opposite side. The ropes carried massive iron buckets up to gigantic stone ovens, where the copper was purified and smelted. The fires burned all night and all day. Midway down that same side of the pit, a vast ledge had been carved out. Stables fronted the ledge, and stone dwellings lined the sides. Helena assumed this was where the mine had originated. The man-made caves ran far back into the cliffs and served as barracks for the prisoners. Helena felt a raging thirst, as though she shared the prisoners' fate.

She gathered with Macarius, Anthony, Cratus, Favian, and Evander atop the rise to survey the mine. The rest of the group held back, clearly shamed by the role they had played in this tragedy. Helena asked, "Why is the mine silent?"

"They knew we were coming," Favian replied hoarsely, as though he shared her thirst.

"What does that mean?"

"They will use the prisoners as hostages," Anthony explained, his features craven. "If we attack, the guards will slaughter them all."

"In any case, a frontal assault would be perilous," Favian said. "The two paths leading to the mine's main ledge are very narrow. We would be forced to fight our way down single file."

"I suspect Severus is waiting for that very moment," Anthony said. "He will attack our rear when we are stretched out and most vulnerable."

Cratus turned and searched the empty road behind them. "I don't see him."

"He's there," Anthony replied, not turning from his survey of the mine.

"How do you know?"

"I can smell him. He carries the odor of death."

Helena declared, 'We will do nothing to endanger the prisoners."

Anthony exchanged a glance with Macarius, who said, "There is perhaps an alternative."

She realized they had been discussing this very moment as they approached the mine. "And that is?"

Anthony replied, "You could speak to them."

"What?"

"Address the soldiers down there. Give them a reason to cross over."

Favian objected, "The ones who did not come back with Evander, they have given up their humanity."

"You do not know the power of our risen Lord to save the doomed and the hopeless," Macarius retorted.

Favian shook his head. "I fear they have descended so far into the pit of bitter despair they hear nothing and think less."

Anthony's response was hesitant, as though he explored the words as he spoke them. "I am only coming to realize just how powerful a voice God has, even when he is silent. He can reach a man lost in sorrow, hiding in a cave of his own making. Even then, God can touch him and make him want to live again."

Helena felt her eyes burn, though she could not say exactly why. "I am not a speaker."

"You are why we are here," Anthony replied simply.

"I have no authority over the soldiers down there."

"It is not your authority that they should obey," Macarius told her.

She turned and surveyed the grim scene. Her voice quaked slightly. "What could I possibly tell them?"

"The truth," Macarius replied.

* * *

At a gesture from Macarius, the others gathered and prayed. The men stood in solemn ranks and bowed their heads as the priest spoke words Helena could scarcely bring herself to hear. She did not so much shut her eyes as clench her entire body. When Macarius went silent, she forced herself to open her eyes, take a deep breath, and step forward until she was perched alone on the rim of the mine.

She did not hesitate. She had always been terrified of speaking in public. She knew if she did not start immediately, she would never be able to do this. The one thought she latched onto as she stared out over the empty mine was *I will not let my friends or my God down.*

Helena's voice sounded half an octave higher than normal to her own ears. The skin of her face and neck felt tight as a drumhead. Her words carried out in the still hot air. "I am Helena. Some call me empress. Others call me augustine. I am neither, though I have been both. I was also once a wife. Now I am not that either. I am nothing, save a servant of the risen Lord. And a messenger of his holy will."

The mine was empty, silent. She spoke to the sun and the heat. Beyond the salt flats, the sea was mirror-smooth. The stone barracks baked alongside the yellow cliff. There was no motion. But she could feel the eyes upon her.

"I have come to this land because I was called. The Lord spoke to me. It was him. I know this, as clearly as I know my own name. He told me to come to Judea, where I would achieve a holy task."

She lifted her hand, holding the parchment high overhead. "This is the first edict my son, the general Constantine, has ever written. It is named for the city where it was penned and signed. The Edict of Milan. It frees all Christians. They are no longer slaves. Their guards are also freed from their odious duties. Do you hear me? Rome frees you!"

A vast sigh rose from the empty yellow pit. It was not a word, nor a shout, nor a cry. A thousand mouths opened and released a burden of fear and tension. The sigh lofted upwards, a soft liberation, gentle as unseen wings.

Helena's voice strengthened. "My Lord told me that I would come here, alone and unguarded, and reveal his power to a dark and despairing world. I did not want to come. Listen well, my people. I asked him to take this duty from me. I was beaten down and I was hurting and I was alone and I was afraid. Yes, afraid! And he said that his power would be revealed through my weakness!"

She dropped her hand to her side and stood staring out over the sun-drenched pit. The heat made the far side tremble. "I ask that you join with me in this holy quest. Unite with me in this divine mission! Come and see the risen Lord perform his miracles! Come with me to Jerusalem!"

CHAPTER 17

The hour before dawn, Helena and her company watched a line of torches descend the path to the beach. Over a hundred prison guards and mine personnel were leaving. Those who departed took everything they could carry with them. Though she had no idea how they might feed those who remained, Helena was not the least bit sorry to watch the sunrise procession abscond with so many of the supplies. There before her stretched a miracle, for Anthony was certain what they saw was the retreat of all their foes.

They remained on the ledge where they had camped above the mine as the galleys lifted sails and carved liquid furrows through the sunrise. Finally, the vessels cleared the rock promontory and turned north, heading toward their allies in Caesarea. Anthony declared, "I want to take a band of armed men down to be certain all those loyal to Damascus have departed."

"I do not agree."

"My lady," he waved a hand at the departing ships. "We have no other way of knowing that they have not planned an ambush."

"We do not enter this arena with might and sword and wrath."

"My lady…"

"We come in the Lord's peace." She did not insist. She did not command. Rather, she asked as a friend would. "And I need to accompany you."

* * *

As they started the descent, she glanced back to where Favian and a number of the troop remained upon the ledge. Anthony walked ahead of them, followed by Cratus and Evander. Their numbers were soon strung out single-file along the steep path.

The prison guards watched in silence as Helena and her group arrived at the broad ledge. The wind was off the land this day, which meant not a breath spilled down to where Helena stood. The air was compressed by the heat and the tension.

Anthony glanced at Evander. A silent communication must have passed between the two men, for Evander stepped forward and shouted hoarsely, "Salute your empress!"

The sound of fists striking leather breastplates was fierce. Helena resisted the urge to correct them, to remind the gathered force that she bore no title. That in fact the word only accentuated everything she had lost. But she decided it did not matter, not really. Not in the face of everything else that this day held.

Anthony turned to her. "My lady?"

She took her time and inspected the troops. Almost all came from outlying territories, mercenaries and conscripts drawn from defeated tribes. Chieftains offered up these men's services as part of Rome's tribute. Helena counted a hundred and twelve of them. All standing at attention. Waiting.

Helena began, "You are commanded to release the prisoners. You will then feed them. When you have fulfilled this final duty, you are dismissed."

The assembled guards stirred as much as trained troops could and still remain at attention. A voice from the back ranks called back, "Where are we to go?"

"That is for you to decide. But this mine is hereby closed. Forever. May its name be wiped from history."

Another called out, "And if we want to stay with you?"

Helena let that question hang in the still air. She had no idea
how to respond. For the danger they faced was very real. And
yet to discuss it somehow seemed to mock the miracle they had
witnessed, when their opposition had marched down to the
seaside and boarded ships and sailed away.

To her astonishment, Anthony demanded of the soldiers, "Will
you walk with your former prisoners as brethren?"

The question was met by utter silence. Evander then added,
"Will you fight to protect them?"

Anthony went on, "Will you give up your life for them?"

There was a long hesitation before a third voice shouted, "In
God's name, we will!"

Favian stepped up beside Helena and said softly, "My lady, I
was wrong to doubt."

Before she could form a proper response, Anthony unfastened
his sword belt and handed it to Evander. He then lifted the leather
breastplate over his head and gave this also to the officer. Evander
must have known this was going to happen, for he motioned to
one of his men, who stepped forward holding a gray robe similar
to what Helena wore. Anthony accepted the robe from Evander
and put it on.

Anthony gave the assembly a long moment to inspect him, a
senior officer dressed in peasant garb. He then told them, "I do
not know why we go to Jerusalem. I do not need to know. Helena
says she has been called to this duty by the Lord Jesus. I accept
this as fact. From this day forward, I will walk alongside her as
a pilgrim. All who wish to join us on this quest are welcome. But
know this. Those who walk with us are no longer prisoner nor
guard. We are all brothers in Christ. Only those who will accept
this as fact, as law, are welcome."

From her other side, Macarius murmured, "Miracle upon
miracle."

Helena gave a single nod and then swallowed hard against the welling of emotions. She would be strong. For them.

When she was certain she could control her voice, she said, "Anthony."

"My lady."

"Release those who are prisoners no longer."

CHAPTER 18

Helena spent the next three days becoming accustomed to her new role. She had never been busier. Or more fulfilled. Even in the midst of sorrow, for they lost two of the former prisoners in that time, Helena knew her life was forever changed, and most certainly, the change was good.

While the officers readied their growing numbers for departure, Helena spent most of her time down at the seafront. Bordering the salt flats was a narrow beach. She and her little team erected open-sided tents, so the sickest among the prisoners could feel the cool breeze and remain shaded from the sun. Some prisoners refused to accept food from the hands of soldiers assigned to tend the cooking pots, which Helena kept simmering all day and night. Some soldiers objected to being used as servants. Helena resolved this in two ways. First, she relied upon troops and former guards who volunteered for the duty, and she did not condemn those who turned away. And those prisoners who distrusted the guards, Helena fed herself. For her, it was a return to her earliest roots. She left behind all the trappings of Rome and became the innkeeper's daughter again. She discovered a divine logic in journeying to the empire's furthest reaches only to arrive back at her beginnings.

The camp had wagons used for transporting copper ore and salt. Anthony and his team filled several with the camp's remaining supplies. Helena scrubbed and boiled blankets and lined other wagons for transporting the former prisoners who remained too ill to walk. All the prisoners begged to come, even those warned they would not survive the journey. Helena was determined to fulfill their final wish.

Each dawn, they gathered for prayer, filling the rim that looked out over the yellow pit. The sun burnished the sea and painted the hillside with a glow that offered hope of a better tomorrow, at least for Helena. Though she rarely spoke at these services, she had the feeling that her presence calmed the lingering hostility between guard and prisoner. Many of the troopers were worried about the future, and many prisoners could not see beyond what they had suffered and all they had lost. Family and health and land and wealth, all gone. They spoke of this to Helena, who listened as she fed and washed and prayed and soothed. She seldom spoke, but her silence became part of her healing balm. She gave it to everyone who asked.

The hour before sunset on the third afternoon, they gathered yet again for a funeral service. Macarius instructed Evander to bang the long metal pipe formerly used as the camp's signal. The soldier struck in slow rhythm, over and over, pausing between each beat, as though it was a great bell announcing the end of struggle, of despair, of strife. Everyone, save the troops on guard duty, walked or were carried down the narrow path. They gathered along the cliffs rising from the salt beds. The sentries along the mine rim looked very small to Helena. As though all earthly threats could scarcely be noticed down here among the people gathered to pray over a newly departed soul.

Small caverns had been dug into the base of the hillside to serve as crypts. Macarius used a mound of gritty untreated salt as an altar table. He said the words and then shared the bread and wine with the gathering. When the service ended, Helena watched those who were healthy climb the paths and return to their duties. In the sunset hour, she knew her anxiety and tainted memories were fading. Her life was simply too full for bitter regret.

That night, for the first time in almost a year, she slept easy.

* * *

Their first night on the Jerusalem road, they held a council of war.

They certainly made a motley collection. Disgraced officers from four different legions sat alongside a newly appointed tribune, one without an army. They were joined by senior guards from an empty mine and six former prisoners who had been appointed elders of the freed community. They were watched over by a priest whose church had been demolished and an empress without a throne. Helena listened as Macarius opened with a prayer and decided she had never felt more at home.

Anthony addressed the former guards officers, "Repeat for the others what you told me."

"Severus came to the mine."

"When?"

"The night before you arrived. He spoke with the senior offi-cers. He ordered them to draw your lot into the paths and onto the ledge. Then he would attack from the rear."

"Just as we suspected," Anthony said.

"He will not give up," Favian said. "He is out there now. I am certain of this."

"There is more," the guards officer said. He was a burly, unkempt fellow, clearly uncomfortable with being a part of this gathering. "He ordered us to leave you and the lady alive. He said he wanted—"

"Enough," Helena said. "We do not need to taint this night with such vile plans."

Anthony asked, "What are your intentions, my lady?"

"The same as always. I go to Jerusalem. I seek to do my Lord's will." She looked around the gathering, meeting the eye of each man in turn. "I did not ask you here to discuss tactics. Our way forward is set. I wanted each of you to understand the risk you take by remaining with us. All of you are free to go. We will see you off with money and supplies."

One of the prisoners said, "They have destroyed my village."

"You can rebuild. We will help."

"How can we be certain the marauders from Damascus will not return?"

"There is no certainty. But if you choose to leave, we will help you. More than that, I cannot say."

She dismissed them. Further discussions would not help. Either they decided to journey with her or they did not. But as the others slipped from the tent, she bade Anthony and the priest remain. Helena took the clay pot from her maid and served them both tea. She asked Anthony, "How many are we?"

"Ninety-three guards, eight hundred twenty former prisoners."

"Ninety-three soldiers," she corrected.

"Only about three dozen have ever known service with a legion," he replied. "The rest are mercenaries who saw this as an easy life."

"And yet they stayed."

"I asked a few. It appears that they were brought to Jesus by those they guarded."

She stared out the open portal at the night. "Why are all the former prisoners coming?"

"Some because they have lost everything and have nowhere else to go. Some because they fear they will be arrested again if they return home. I suppose we will lose many of them along the way, as they become more accustomed to their freedom."

"And the rest?"

This time, Macarius was the one who spoke. "They seek a miracle."

"I have had heard it often enough to accept it as truth," Anthony agreed. "They believe you are here to do great things. They hope for a miracle in their lives. They wish to come and..."

"Yes? And what?"

"And witness God's presence," Macarius responded. "More than that they cannot say. How could they? You have not shared with us what your mission is."

"It is God's mission, not mine."

Anthony said, "They will do what you ask of them. As will I and all the other men."

She inspected the officer's robe of gray homespun, which was all he had worn since the morning on the ledge. "And here you are, accompanying me as a pilgrim."

"I share their trust in you."

"Has the Lord answered your prayer? Has he given you a purpose?"

"Not exactly." Anthony examined the cup in his hands. "I had lost everything I ever cared for in this life. My wife and my son were taken from me. I came with neither purpose nor desire to live."

"And now?"

"I want to see this through. I feel..."

"Go on."

"I feel closer to my wife than I have since she departed. I have returned to the altar. I pray. For the moment, that is enough."

"My son would be proud of you. As am I." Helena walked over and closed the tent-flaps. She turned back and said, "It is time I share with you my vision."

* * *

The vision had come to her at sunrise, nine days after being expelled from her home. She had lost the home plus every shred of the future she had assumed was hers to claim. She was accompanied on the road by Cratus, who had brought her the articles of divorce. She was traveling to her son's military camp, and word had filtered north that Constantine's army faced a battle they could not win. She was bereft, she was alone, and she walked toward her own doom.

That morning Helena had offered a few dry words of prayer before readying herself to go through the motions of another empty day. Then the encounter had begun.

There had been no sense of separating herself from her surroundings. She had known vividly where she was, every instant. It had simply no longer mattered. Nothing did, except the vision. There had been no room for anything else.

In her vision, Helena watched as the cross had been levered up, up, up, into a desolate sky. Then, with a great booming *thunk,* it slipped down into the earth. She was positioned behind the cross, which was good, for she knew that if she had stood where she could see the Lord Jesus, in his final hours of mortal agony, she would have perished. She did not think this. She knew.

Helena watched as the sky darkened, and the Savior breathed his last, and the world became blanketed by gloom. She knew the shroud that wrapped itself across the sky was a mere reflection of the Father's sorrow. What Helena felt was not her own remorse, though she knew she was as guilty as any for Jesus's being sent to die upon that sorrowful ground. She glimpsed into the Father's own grief. Though the world would be brought to him by this act, though it was necessary, though he had himself willed this into being, still the Lord of all lamented. And all the world with him. Helena most of all.

When it was over and Helena was once again back in her tent and struggling to recover, the room was filled by a Presence. And it was then that God spoke to her.

The Lord gave her a direct challenge. And she would do it. For him, and for the world. Because he asked.

* * *

As she spoke, Helena once again relived the encounter. The act of sharing created a bond as powerful and vivid as the instant she had heard God's voice. She studied the two men and knew with utter certainty they felt the same. Her words were a door through which the Spirit entered their tent.

When she finished, she sat and waited. She recalled that dawn, the worst of her life. She had lost almost everything. Her life had been reduced to ashes and danger. She had no home, no money, no title, and her son was probably not going to survive the coming battle. She saw nothing ahead of her save shame and regret and her own demise.

Which was when the Presence had revealed to her a different destiny.

Helena had no idea how long the three of them sat, bound together by far more than words. A minute, an hour, the very concept of time held no meaning. The Holy Spirit had breathed upon them, and they together had moved *beyond* time. They saw *beyond* the world. And they heard the unspoken Voice.

Together.

Finally, Macarius shifted himself down to his knees and said the words that echoed through her life, "Let us go to the Lord in prayer."

: CHAPTER 19 :

:

Helena trudged along the Jerusalem road. The road leading inland was not much used, for Jerusalem remained a mostly destroyed city. All Roman traffic ran from Caesarea through Samaria, around the Sea of Galilee then north and east toward Damascus. Around mid-morning, Anthony and Macarius moved up alongside her. Anthony began, "We were wondering if now might be a good time to speak of what lies ahead."

"I would welcome your company."

Anthony waved to Favian. The scouts officer slipped off his mount, handed the reins to a guard, and joined them. Anthony said, "Macarius has not been back to Jerusalem in ten years, not since Severus took his family and destroyed his church. Favian has visited the city twice since then."

Helena asked the scouts captain, "What was it like?"

"Very moving to walk the same streets as our Savior," Favian replied. "But also very sad."

"How so?"

"The general who fought the Judeans in their second uprising was Hadrian. After defeating their army, he turned much of Jerusalem to rubble. Only the eastern portion, away from the Temple Mount, remains inhabited, and only by Romans. This portion was renamed Aelia Capitolina. Less than two thousand Romans live there now. And no Judeans at all. They are still banished, a century after their defeat. Hadrian erected a temple to

Venus on the city's highest hill, my lady. And on Temple Mount he built another dedicated to Saturn."

Macarius took up the account, "I know nothing about the city's earlier layout. All I have to go on are legends and secondhand accounts. Most Romans who dwell there care little for the past."

Anthony went on, "My lady, whatever it is you intend to accomplish once we arrive, we will need the help of outsiders. Favian has an idea."

Favian pointed back behind them, to the juncture where the Jerusalem road separated from the main north-south route. "The Judean scholars now live in Bnei Brak. The village lies half a day's ride south, near the port of Jaffa. A teacher named Akiba ben Joseph set up a school there after Solomon's Temple was destroyed. They say it is the future of Judaism."

"You have been there?"

"Once. When I first arrived in Judea, I served as royal messenger. I was sent to deliver a letter from the governor. The rabbis would not receive me." He scowled at the memory. "I was forced to leave the parchment in the dust. They refused to touch it until I was gone. They said to deal with me would render them unclean."

She inspected the two officers. They were both very striking, and yet quite different. Anthony was her son's type of soldier, strong and silent and solid. Even dressed in gray homespun, Anthony gave the impression of strength like some ancient tree, deeply rooted in the earth. Favian, on the other hand, carried himself with the suppleness of a dueling sword. His eyes were the color of old copper, his hair one shade darker. No doubt he had a very winning smile. But she had never seen it. And he was most certainly not smiling now. In fact, the man's gaze reflected a deep wound. Helena asked, "Anthony, do you carry the gold?"

In reply, he handed her a soft deerskin pouch. Helena fished out two coins and handed them to Favian. "Take this to the Judeans.

Tell them we go to Jerusalem. If they would agree to join us, we will give them more gold and grant them permission to resettle the city."

He stared at the gold. "To a group of impoverished scholars this will be a king's ransom."

"They probably won't come for the gold," Helena said. "But I hope they will come for the city."

Favian slipped the coins into his belt and started away. He took hold of his horse's reins, gripped the pommel, and hesitated.

Helena knew what he was to ask and knew as well it would be impossible to answer. But just the same she said, "You may speak, Officer Favian."

"What was it like, my lady? Having God speak to you."

She studied this man, and in that brief connection, she saw how much he had endured. The agony that had come from his declaration of faith. The lies he had told, the misery he had known. And yet even now, there burned in his dark gaze the glimmer of hope. And she knew, with the utter certainty of wisdom gifted from above, that if she was to succeed, she needed to bare her own soul. And give him the grace of sharing her quest.

Helena replied, "There has only been one experience on this good earth as intense as then. And that was the day I gave birth to my son. All else fades in comparison. It was a glimpse beyond the veil, into the heart of the One we serve."

He bowed, an officer to his empress. "Thank you, my lady."

"God keep you safe on your journey, Officer Favian."

Favian leapt into the saddle and wheeled his mount around. "What should I tell the Judeans if they ask why it is so important for them to join us?"

"Tell them the truth," Helena replied. "Say they could well be the answer to a prayer I had not yet even formed."

: CHAPTER 20 :

:

When they halted at sunset, Helena walked the long line of wagons, speaking with the sick and the elderly. She brought them water, she checked on the cooking pots, she comforted those in pain.

After the evening service, she approached Macarius and asked if they could talk. They settled by the roadside fire where a blackened kettle of troopers' tea constantly simmered. Macarius sipped from a tin mug of the thick, heavily sweetened brew, and said, "Favian came to me before dawn. He told me he suffered from a memory that assaulted him with the force of enemy marauders. I asked if I might share this with you and Anthony. I told him you both would know what it meant to be afflicted by recollections."

Helena watched the sparks rise up to join with the distant stars. "I understand all too well."

"He related the day the edict from Damascus was nailed to the barracks wall. The so-called caesar ordered each new Christian prisoner to be scarred for life. The guards were commanded to alternate between blinding one eye, slashing one ankle-tendon, branding one thigh, and cutting off one hand. Any soldier who refused to carry out the order was to be scourged to death. Him and all his family, down to the youngest infant."

Helena turned and looked back to where the former guards clustered around their own fire while a few of their number moved from one wagon to the next, offering food and water to the injured prisoners. "Those poor men."

"Favian told me that his reaction was one of relief. Because he was a scout, he escaped having to perform these ghastly acts. But now, he feels that he is as guilty as those who wielded the knife and the ax and the branding iron. He knows that was the fate I suffered. He came asking my forgiveness."

"Which you gave him, I hope and pray," Helena said.

"Of course I did. That is not the point. Afterward, I held him as he wept like a broken-hearted child. And that is not the point either." Macarius leaned in closer. "When we were done, we discovered Anthony had been waiting to speak with us. He shared your vision with Favian. He described our concerns over how we might locate places from the time of King Herod. Do you see?"

"I… No, I don't…"

"Through Anthony, through you, God has sent Favian a message. He is telling that young man that not only is he forgiven but that it is time for him to look beyond. To accept that there is a holy purpose at work here, and Favian is invited to take part." Macarius leaned back. "You spoke because it was time. And in so doing, you have given that young man the most precious of God's gifts. A reason to live."

* * *

The trek from the coastal road to the Jerusalem foothills took three days. It should have been done in half that, but the former prisoners could only walk so fast or for so long. Helena insisted upon holding to a pace that all could manage. Her tone made it clear that she would not be hurried, not even when they caught sight of the massive dust cloud on the horizon, which the soldiers were certain meant Severus had gathered more men and was preparing for an attack.

With each sunrise, they greeted more new arrivals. Evander and several of the scouts had taken to riding out each day, carrying the message of Constantine's edict to outlying villages. In response, more and more people joined them. And each evening, as they shared the sacraments, many newcomers wept when they accepted the cup from Helena's hands.

At dawn on the fourth day, the climb into the hills started. Helena's legs and feet complained, of course, but she was well used to that by now. It was the ache in her heart that left her so burdened she could scarcely keep up with Macarius on his donkey. They had buried two more souls before setting out. The former prisoners had both passed away peacefully in the night, and the simple roadside service had been both poignant and moving. But for Helena, it had driven home all the uncertainties over this ever-growing band of people who gathered around her. "I'm not Moses," she complained to the priest.

"No. Most certainly not."

"I haven't been commanded to lead the afflicted out of Egypt."

"Quite right." Macarius squinted into the distance.

"I am already in the Promised Land, and so are they."

"Yes indeed."

"I was called to go to Jerusalem. I was told to go alone."

"Were you now?"

"God didn't say..." She glanced over. "Are you paying me the slightest bit of attention?"

Macarius was turned around now, peering back into the flatlands they were leaving behind. "Someone is coming."

"Of *course* they're coming. That's the whole *point*. They are *always* coming."

"No. Someone else. I'm almost certain..."

Before she could ask him to complete the sentence, Anthony came rushing back. "Soldiers."

The bishop continued to squint at the horizon. "Just as I thought."

"A lot of soldiers."

By now, the entire group had halted. Helena pulled the donkey around so Macarius did not risk falling off while he craned about and searched. "All I see is dust."

"Every now and then I catch a glimpse of...There! Did you see?"

"Yes." She did, too. The sunlight had glinted off something metallic. Actually, rather a lot of them. Pinpricks of light that danced in the distance. A forest of spears. Coming their way. "What are we to do?"

Neither man spoke. Helena felt the fears well up, until she had to force herself to keep a calm tone. "Answer me."

"I don't think they are our foes," Anthony decided. Somewhere in the distance, one of the guards bellowed the alarm. Without turning his face from the horizon, Anthony roared, "Stand down!"

The air weaved in a tantalizing dance. Legionnaires scrambled up to stand beside him. Helena squinted into the distance. "Tell me what I am supposed to be seeing!"

"The horsemen are riding to either side of those who walk," Anthony said.

"This means precisely what?"

"If they were entering into battle, some of the mounted troops would take a forward position," Anthony replied. "The scouts would approach at a gallop, catching glimpses of how our men are stationed."

"Perhaps they feel no need," said one of the other soldiers, clearly unwilling to give into hope. "We are too small a troop to bother."

"There are many dead officers who misjudged an opposing force," Anthony replied. He pointed to the approaching horde. "Look at their sword arms."

By now, many of the soldiers had gathered on the road. Another man shouted, "Their hands are empty!"

"And their shields are slung on their backs," Anthony replied.

Behind him, he heard Macarius laugh out loud.

Anthony yelled, "*Scout!*"

"Here, sir!"

To Helena's eyes, the man looked impossibly young. But he carried himself with the same lighthearted ease as Favian. Anthony pointed in their direction. "Ride out. If they are believers, welcome them."

"It will be done, sir!"

"Do not put yourself in harm's way for what could well be a fool's errand," Anthony warned.

The young scout tightened the chin-strap to his plumed helmet, which caught the sun and glowed like burnished bronze. "That is the first time a general has ever expressed concern for my well-being."

Anthony motioned him onward. "Go and greet them in God's name."

Macarius watched the young scout gallop down the road and head across the yellow plain. "There are stories throughout the Scriptures of battles that were never fought at all, save by the hand of God. What would you call a man who serves the Lord through avoiding conflict?"

When Anthony's only response was to continue watching the scout disappear into the shimmering light, Macarius said, "A hero is what I would call such a man. A hero for the Lord our God."

: CHAPTER 21 :

:

Gradually, Anthony's legion took form.

Four hundred legionnaires, five hundred, six, Helena did not bother to count. Some came with wagons filled with produce. Others arrived half-starved.

And all brought word of the army beyond the horizon.

Newly arrived officers reported that the consul in Caesarea had sent Constantine's edict to Damascus. In response, Maximinus had ordered Severus to gather an army and wipe Helena's entire band off the face of the earth. Helena listened as the officers described how word spread among the troops like wildfire. That Constantine's own mother brought word of the dawning of a new era. One where Christians were no longer hunted down and killed. One where faith in Jesus was no longer a crime.

Helena listened to them, recalled the words of her vision, and shivered with awe.

Anthony took charge of supplies, sending out foraging parties made up of soldiers and prisoners alike. In each village where a Christian community had managed to survive, money was left to rebuild their church. Everywhere they went, Anthony's men were warned of a great army beyond the horizon.

And all that day and the next, more and more people joined them.

They climbed into the central Judean highlands along the same route used by King David. The ancient road meandered up a gradual incline, rising through ochre hills carved into artwork by eons of desert winds. Their pace remained set by the wagons and by the slowest of the former prisoners. At every bend in the road, Helena turned and looked back, as did most of the company. They had grown to a staggering size. They coursed down the road for over two miles. And still more people came. She watched as families scurried along goat-tracks that ran through the dry hills. Knowing the danger, yet joining them just the same. Many soldiers claimed their growing numbers kept the attackers at bay. Helena found no need to respond.

Occasionally, a horseman would be seen surveying them from a rise. Newly arriving troops reported that the Damascus governor had placed prices on their heads. A thousand gold denarii for Helena, fifty for the head of every officer who had deserted caesar's army. For this was how they were classed. Deserters all.

On the second day since entering the highlands, they made camp just four miles from Jerusalem. In the distance rose the Roman coliseum built on the city's western ridge. They could have reached Jerusalem before sunset if they had pushed, but another prisoner died at mid-afternoon. Helena held the woman's hand until the very last. Anthony stood alongside her the entire time.

Afterward, as they watched a clutch of soldiers and prisoners dig the grave together, Macarius joined them. "News of your actions have been passed from voice to voice down the curving road."

Helena found it difficult to focus upon anything other than this most recent loss. She had not even known the woman's name but yet felt the absence deep in her bones. "I'm sorry, what?"

The priest waved a hand back to where people still tramped off the road and entered their camp, set in a narrow valley with a spring at its heart. "Everyone talks of nothing else. How an empress and her newly appointed tribune held the death watch for a former prisoner of the realm."

Anthony's features had been turned hollow by the long hours. "We could not save her."

"No, and now she rests in our Lord's embrace." Macarius limped forward, gripped the soldier's arm, and turned him about. "Look down there. Tell me what you see."

His voice rasped as he echoed Helena's unspoken concerns. "A countless band we cannot protect."

"No, my dear friend. I'm sorry, but you are wrong. What you see are a growing number of believers, drawn by the power of our shared faith."

"But I could well be leading them to their deaths!"

"And if they remain hiding in their villages, would that give them a better chance? Listen to what I am saying. They have witnessed a miracle this day. A woman who had been sentenced to the mines was cared for with tenderness to the last breath. She is now mourned by all, and yet there is such joy. Yes, joy!"

"I feel none of it," Anthony replied.

"And yet you should. Why? Because you and this fine woman standing beside you are living symbols of the faith that binds us all."

Helena looked out past the grave and the shrouded body, down the length of the valley, to where the last wagon slowly made its way into the camp. The grassy field was completely covered. As she studied the gathering, she realized they all held one thing in common.

They were all waiting.

Anthony asked, "Why are you telling me this?"

"Because you need to address them."

"Me?" The officer was pushed back a step. "I have never spoken to anyone but soldiers in my entire life."

"They need to hear from you," Macarius persisted. The soldiers and the villagers and the prisoners alike. The officer who shares the lady's pilgrimage, who has given up his fine uniform and wears gray homespun. Who cares for them. Who *leads* them."

"Helena is our leader."

"And you are her first officer. It is time, Anthony. The Lord calls to you. Stand before these people and tell them why."

Helena said quietly, "The pastor is correct."

Macarius did not wait for Anthony's reply. Instead, he turned and called in a voice too great for his wizened frame, "Let us gather together!"

At a gesture from the older man, Anthony joined Macarius on a stone ledge that jutted above the grave, perhaps twice the height of a man. The priest waved both hands in the motion of an embrace. "I ask that everyone move closer." Then, "Come closer still."

Then Macarius gestured to Anthony and stepped back, leaving him there, looking out over a sea of upturned faces.

Anthony hesitated a long moment and then declared, "I want to live!"

Macarius looked down at Helena then. The sun was setting behind the priest, so it was hard to make out his expression. But Helena thought she saw him smile.

"For ten long months, I have wanted to die," Anthony told the gathering. "I lost my wife as she gave birth to my stillborn son. I dug their graves with my own hands, and I laid my own heart in the earth with them. I came to Judea looking for a place to breathe my last and join them in the other world."

The wind was silenced by the setting sun. Helena felt the sweat trickle down her face. She listened as Anthony went on, "I have learned there are more important things than this life we share, here in the Jerusalem highlands. I have been given a glimpse of something greater. I do not understand much of it. I do not need to. I am a soldier. But this I do know. For as long as I am given the chance to draw another breath, I will march in service to the Lord Jesus Christ."

Anthony waved a hand, taking in the entire gathering. "Upon the road, I have seen how we walk clan with clan, trooper with trooper. We seek the comfort of people we know, and who know us. But this day I have stood and watched as together we dug a grave. And that is what I want to ask of you. That tomorrow we do not enter Jerusalem as troopers, or former prisoners, or clansmen, or villagers. We are here to fulfill a divine mission. To succeed, we must join together.

"I ask that each of you select a person who was once your enemy. Turn to them now and offer them the blessing and grace of our Lord Jesus Christ."

Anthony then turned to Macarius and embraced him. Helena could see the scars where the hot poker had been applied to the priest's eye. Then Helena turned and embraced someone, she was not sure who, for by then her vision was veiled by tears.

: CHAPTER 22 :

:

The camp was ready to depart well before dawn. While the stars were still visible in the western reaches, Macarius stood upon the ledge and prayed over them. The silence held as Helena and Anthony and Macarius led the procession forward. At Helena's request, the wagons holding the sickest were moved to the very front. Anthony and Macarius accompanied Helena at the fore. The priest rode the same donkey that had carried him since Caesarea. As they wound around the first bend in the road, Helena heard Macarius say to Anthony, "They have a name for you now."

"Who is that?"

The priest waved a hand at the mass of people snaking slowly along behind them. "I overheard them speaking last night. They call you the pilgrim general. The man in gray. They would follow you anywhere."

They made their base upon the Mount of Olives. Helena found the location to be ideal. The ancient grove offered shade, and the ground was covered by a leafy blanket of silver leaves. The wind laced through the gnarled limbs, whispering a welcome.

Before them was the Valley of Kidron, and beyond that, Jerusalem. The old city crowned a long sloping ridge. Even in its decrepit state, Jerusalem held a timeless glory. The stones glowed in the afternoon light, as though some heavenly mineral had been mixed together with the mortar. The gates were gone, the encircling wall was torn down in places, and the city was mostly rubble. Even so, its spirit lived on.

The air was soon filled with smoke from numerous cooking fires. Vast iron kettles began emitting fragrances. As the sun began its slow descent, Helena sought out Anthony and Macarius. "I feel it is time that I share my mission with everyone."

"Wonderful," Macarius declared. "Many of course know part or all of your story. But none have heard it from your lips."

"Will you both please stand beside me?"

"Always, my lady," the general replied.

Macarius echoed, "It would be my honor."

So it was that the three of them climbed upon the narrow knoll that rose at the crest of the hill. They faced the grove, so that those gathered could look over the city that rose in luminous grandeur behind them.

They were so many. The grove covered a flat parkland and then sloped down to a trio of ledges. All were filled by people.

Helena said, "The Lord came to me in a vision."

Her voice carried well. This day held no space for her fear of crowds. All she heard in her voice was conviction. "God came during a time so dark I was blind to the rising sun. My husband had divorced me so he might consort with his young maids. My only son was battling for his life in a distant land. Few believed he would survive, for Constantine faced two armies, both far larger than his own force. I prayed until I was too exhausted to pray any more. I fell asleep. The next dawn, God came to me."

The people were packed in so tight the former prisoners and the former guards were massed as one. They stood silent and unmoving, their faces upturned to the empress and the general and the priest in gray. Helena continued, "God said that not only would my son survive, but Constantine would alter the course of history. He would declare Rome to be a Christian empire. And I was to come to Jerusalem as part of this holy quest. I was to come and recover the symbol of our Lord's sacrifice."

A soft murmur filled the grove, gentle as the wind rustling the silver leaves. Helena waited until they were silent once more before continuing, "When my holy encounter ended, I prayed that I would receive a sign that this vision was real. I prayed and fasted until word came of my son's victory at the Milvian Bridge. And with that news came a letter from Constantine himself. In it, he told me of a vision he had received on the dawn of the battle, when Jesus had spoken to him and said this would mark the day of great victory. My son was given a sign of the Lord's hand upon this hour. On the sun, Constantine saw a symbol, the two Greek letters making the name of Christ, *chi* and *rho*, were fashioned into one, forming a holy cross. Constantine heard a voice tell him to wear the sign upon his breast."

She beheld them for a long moment and then finished, "That sign came to him the same dawn as my own vision."

* * *

The next day they were awoken by drums.

By the time Helena emerged from her tent, every soldier was already on his feet. Helena understood why. The sound was unmistakable. The drumbeat was the same throughout the Roman empire, a rattling call to arms and war. Her son had once confessed that he often dreamed of the sound and woke up drenched with sweat from the thrill and the fear of the battle to come.

Helena gathered with the others at the ledge and stared across the valley. The wrecked city walls were festooned with soldiers in armor. Their spears were topped with flags that fluttered with gay defiance in the morning wind.

And there at its center was a tall soldier whose golden breast-plate gleamed like a second sun.

"They have put their entire force on this side of the city," Anthony said. "Either they expect a frontal assault, or they intend to lead one against us."

Helena turned away, closed her eyes, and prayed. It was hard to shut out the rising clamor. But she knew this was no longer about human plans. Even now, when faced with a battle in the making, she sought guidance. All the eyes were upon her as she raised her head and declared, "We will not fight."

Anthony hesitated and then nodded.

It was left to Evander to ask the question. "What are we to do if they attack?"

"We pray," Anthony replied. "Pray, and wait for God to show us the way."

Helena did not allow herself to either return to the knoll or even stare across the valley for the rest of that long, hot day. At the priest's suggestion, she and Anthony joined him, and together they fasted. They sat in the grove by Helena's tent. They read the Scriptures, and they prayed.

The day slipped by. The sun crawled from one horizon to the other. She had never been good at fasting. Yet this day she found a soft delight in the long hours. The time was not wasted. It simply moved to a different cadence. As though they were not merely turning away from food but rather from everyday life. They sat because there was no need to do anything, save wait upon God.

At sunset, the wind quieted. When they gathered for the evening service, the entire camp seemed infected by the stillness that filled Helena's soul. The gathering was so silent she could hear the harsh commands and clank of metal across the valley.

Macarius did not speak once during the service. He lifted the cup and the bread, he distributed the loaf, he shut his eyes, and then it was over. The camp watched the three of them return to the gnarled tree in front of Helena's tent. There was no sound.

Not a baby, nor a dog, nor a bird. The world held its breath. The night grew very cold. And the mist gathered.

When Helena awoke at dawn, the fog was so thick she could not see her hand in front of her face. Even the drums across the valley were silenced. Then out of the gray half-light came a voice she instantly recognized. It belonged to a young scouts officer who had lost the ability to ever smile again, or so it had seemed to her as he had ridden away from them, out into the yellow wasteland.

"Who can see anything in this soup? I've been a scout for my entire adult life, and I can't even find my own feet!"

Helena rose to her feet and cried, "Favian, is that you?"

"It is indeed, my lady!"

"Cratus, can you find the scout?"

"Aye, he's right here before me."

The mist reluctantly parted, and two soldiers took form. Cratus held Favian's horse by the reins, leading them as he would a child on a pony. "Though how he could call himself a scout when he can't even find his own empress is a wonder."

Anthony stepped up beside Helena and demanded, "Where on earth have you been?"

"Doing as I was ordered by the lady here. And I'm glad I did not know what a bother it would be." Favian slid from his horse with the grace of a man born to dance. He knelt in the earth before her. "Greetings, my lady."

"Rise, Favian." Helena found her smile could not be extinguished by the cold, gray dawn. "We have been praying for a miracle. Have you arrived as God's holy messenger?"

"I have been called many things in my short years, my lady. But never that." His features were stretched thin with fatigue, and the shadows were still there, yet he somehow found the strength to grin. "But I like the sound of that title."

Helena allowed herself to hope that a true healing had indeed begun. "You bring glad tidings. I can see that much in your face."

"I have brought you seven rabbis of Bnei Brak, my lady. Though whether they will be of any use is another matter."

Anthony asked again, "What delayed your return?"

"A council of rabbis rules their little village. They sit beneath a great tree all day and argue. They stop to pray and eat, and then they argue some more. Three days and nights they quarreled before they decided that they would send some of their own to speak with you."

Helena demanded, "Where are they now?"

Favian waved off to his left. "The other side of the road, mistress. They claim it would defile them to enter our camp."

"Macarius."

"My lady?"

"Go and welcome them in our name. See to their needs. Ask if I might be permitted to speak with them."

"As you wish, my lady." But when Anthony started to follow, the priest halted him with, "In this matter, I will be better served with a former prisoner as my escort."

CHAPTER 23

Wh](%20)hile they waited for Macarius to return, Favian ate and described his meeting with the rabbis. Helena listened to how they had refused to let him enter their compound, how they forced him to stand in the dust beyond the wall, how they did not offer him either food or drink, how he was ordered to leave the gold by his feet and walk away. How they kept him waiting a day and a night and through most of the next day as well, while they argued among themselves. And yet what Helena heard most of all was the sound of a soul coming back to life.

The fog did not so much disperse as rise grudgingly, until the camp rested beneath a sullen blanket. After Favian finished eating, Helena and Anthony led the scouts officer to the ledge. Favian stared across the valley and took in the spears lining the Jerusalem walls. "Is he there?"

"Severus?" Anthony shrugged. "He hasn't come over and introduced himself. But I caught sight of a golden breastplate."

Evander joined them and added, "One of the officers told me Severus leads all the men the consul could spare. Almost half a legion."

"I heard that too," Anthony confirmed. "And he's armed now with a writ placing the Jerusalem garrison under his command."

"Well, it's good these new men have bolstered our forces," Favian said. "What preparations have you made?"

Anthony continued to stare across the valley. "We fast."

The scouts officer rounded on him. "But they could have sent forces out to hem us in from behind."

"Did you see any?"

"No, but in that fog I could have passed within a hand's breadth and missed them entirely. Surely you've sent out riders to survey the road."

"No scouts have been sent out since we arrived on the Olive Mount."

"We are fasting," Helena confirmed. "And we pray."

Favian looked from one to the other. Helena waited for further protests, when Cratus added, "And I fast with her."

"As do I," Evander said. "Along with many others."

"Perhaps half the camp," Anthony said.

"More," Cratus responded. "Much more."

"I never was much for going without food. I hold to the soldier's creed. I eat when it's there, sleep when I can, fight when I must. And always watch my back," said Favian.

"These are uncommon times," Anthony replied. "I have prayed over this. I feel at peace with our actions."

"We trust in God," Evander agreed.

Favian made a sour face. "Am I to fast with you, then?"

Helena resisted the sudden urge to embrace them all. "You are to do as God wills. Nothing less, and nothing more."

*   *   *

When Macarius finally invited her to join him and the rabbis, Helena asked Anthony to accompany her. As they arrived at the olive grove's southern fringe, she found the rabbis had established a miniature camp of their own. They were dark-robed and bearded and narrow and suspicious. The youngest was in his thirties, and the eldest was a gray-bearded man who was as gnarled and bent as the olive branches overhead. But his voice was strong enough, as he proved when he saw Anthony approaching and called, "Take away a Roman soldier's weapons, garb him in homespun, and he is still a killer of Jews!"

Helena protested, "This is my friend and protector."

"Defiler of holy places! Murderer of innocents! Keep away!"

Helena disliked it but replied, "As you wish. May I approach?"

The men squinted angrily. Two muttered beneath their breath. The elder waved them to silence and asked Macarius, "This is the one of whom you spoke? The empress who has cast aside her crown?"

"I gave up nothing," Helena corrected. "It was taken from me. By a husband who preferred young maids to fulfilling his wedding vows."

The elder gnawed on the fringe of his beard. "You are this honest in all your dealings?"

"With God as my judge, I try to be."

"What is it you want from us?"

"One thing and one thing only. May I enter your camp?" But when three of the rabbis began muttering and flapping their black-robed arms like crows, Helena lowered herself onto the gnarled root of a neighboring tree. "I seek the path Jesus of Nazareth took to his death."

When they saw she would not stand upon ceremony, the rabbis stilled, and the elder said, "Go on."

"On the night Jesus was taken, he gathered with his disciples and ate a final meal. He was then dragged to the residence of the high priest, and from there to Herod's palace, and finally to the palace of Pontius Pilate himself. There he was scourged. Afterward, he was forced to carry his cross from Pilate's residence to the hill known as Golgotha, the place of woe and doom. There he was crucified. I seek to follow this route. But Jerusalem lies mostly in ruins. The city is ringed by hills and ridges and valleys. I have no way of knowing which hill is Golgotha or which road the

Teacher was forced to walk. I ask you to assist me."

"This is why you journeyed to Jerusalem?" The elder seemed genuinely perplexed. "To follow the way of a Judean's death? One laid out by you Romans?"

"It is." Helena found herself intensely calm in the face of this hostility. Nor did she feel any need to point out the role the Judeans had played in the Nazarene's death. "In return, I offer you freedom to return to your city."

"It is no longer *my* city." The elder spat the words. "You have stolen it away! Stolen! You have even robbed us of its name! Aelia Capitolina, you call this place!"

"Jerusalem it was, and so it shall be once more."

The elder stood bent over his staff, both hands kneading the polished surface. "Why should I believe this? You yourself have said you have no power."

"My son is legate and has been invited to become caesar, though there are many who oppose him. I have been granted the authority to issue edicts in his name."

Anthony watched the elder turn and stare at the city. The other rabbis did likewise. Their features were gaunt with the longing of ages.

When the elder turned back, his eyes blazed with yearning. "Your kind have erected an abomination upon our holiest place. They have desecrated the Temple Mount!"

Helena stared across the valley. The structure was clear enough. Beyond the ruined wall and the empty gate stood the broad stone plaza of Temple Mount. It was wide as a plain, and even on this gray day, the stone shone with an otherworldly wonder. At its center, in the place of Solomon's Temple, stood a very different structure. The new temple was dedicated to Saturn, leading deity of the Roman gods. It was open-sided and wreathed in smoke from the bronze incense-stands ringing the sacrificial altar.

Helena rose to her feet. "Thank you for coming and for granting me this audience."

The elder narrowed his gaze, as though searching for an insult. "What are you going to do?"

"You have every reason to disbelieve anything I say," Helena replied. "I am going to earn your trust."

CHAPTER 24

While Helena and Macarius were still with the rabbis, Anthony left the grove and took the road down into the valley. He had scarcely passed the last tree when he heard footsteps racing to catch up. Favian demanded, "And where do you think you're going?"

"You are ordered back to camp."

"Sorry. My hearing's just gone bad." Favian fell into step beside him. "Dangerous place for a walk alone, if you ask me."

Another pair of feet scrambled to catch up, and Evander demanded, "Where are we off to now?"

"The general isn't saying," Favian said readily. "I suppose he's decided it's a good day for a stroll."

"Odd, that, especially since he also hasn't eaten since yesterday."

"What, you're still fasting?"

"Helena continues to pray for guidance. I follow her lead." Anthony replied. "And you both are being insolent."

"Wouldn't be right to let our commanding officer go off wandering alone," Favian replied.

"Especially when his mind might be weakened from lack of food," Evander agreed.

"My head is fine. And I was hoping for a bit of solitude..."

Anthony stopped talking because another score of men came scrambling down the path toward them, soldiers all. Cratus saluted Anthony and said, "The old priest ordered us to make sure you didn't catch a spear."

Favian beckoned the newcomers into a semblance of order. "All right, sire. You just go ahead and have your little solitary wander."

Anthony accepted the inevitable with ill grace. They descended to the valley floor and turned north, off the road and into the defile that rimmed the base of the city wall. Soldiers along the ruined city wall marked their passage. When Anthony glanced back, he saw how his own soldiers had now gathered at the grove's border and tracked their movements. The result was a mobile stand-off. The city's forces dared not attack, not with so many troops watching from the opposite ridge.

Anthony had no idea where he was going. He had simply wanted to go out for a walk while Helena and Macarius were still busy with the rabbis. To see if he could find God in the valley's heat. Or rather, if God would find him.

Instead, here he was, marching along with an array of troops tromping along behind him, with hundreds more observing his every step from two different ridges.

He was about to call a halt when he noticed movement in the grove ahead.

The valley floor was like much of the desert they had passed through, rocky and desolate and creased by countless trails. Here and there rose stone tombs, some big as houses and so ancient they might well have grown from the stony soil. Where the tombs ended, a grove of stunted desert pines massed about a small spring. And amidst those pines he saw movement.

"Stay well back," Anthony ordered.

This time, the men obeyed. For the figure who approached them waved a tattered rag in one outstretched hand. The hand itself was wrapped in old cloth. It was a sign every man among them knew and dreaded. Here in the desolate valley lived a community of lepers.

Anthony felt the shiver of fear course through his empty belly and forced his legs to carry him forward. He stopped two paces from the leper, who did the same. Only then did he realize he faced a woman.

"We have no food," the woman whimpered. "Our spring has gone dry. We have no water."

"We can give you both," Anthony replied. "How many are you?"

The young woman twisted her head, as though disbelieving what she had heard. "You will give?"

"Food and water," Anthony confirmed. "How many—"

"Twenty-seven." The woman trembled in her eagerness. "We were thirty, but three died."

The voice he heard belonged to a person younger than himself. Which made the scabs and scars even harder to accept. "We will leave supplies here in this spot later today." He pointed beyond the stunted grove. "Where does the valley lead?"

"It runs part-way around the old wall."

"And these valleys I see leading away from the city, why are there no trails?"

"All six enter the hills, but they run nowhere."

Anthony nodded. It was as he suspected. He glanced up at the soldiers now massed around the old fortress wall directly above them. Still they made no threatening move. As though some greater hand held them fast. Anthony started to turn away but then asked, "Do you know the Lord Jesus?"

The woman cringed, as though a wrong answer would cost her the promised food. "I...is he a Roman, sire?"

"Far from it." Anthony started to explain, but he quickly sensed that the woman's desperate need made her deaf to all but her hunger and thirst. "I will return with the food. Or another will come in my place. I ask you to listen to the words."

But instead of rejoining his men, Anthony started up the slope toward the hole in the city wall. When Favian called out, he replied, "Stand back!"

He undid his belt and set his dirk on a rock. He lifted the cloth belt as he would a flag of truce and approached within hailing distance. The men along the wall watched him with the resolve of trained soldiers. Anthony spied a single subaltern, no other officers. He called out, "I am the tribune Anthony. I serve under the General Constantine. I come to Jerusalem in peace. As a pilgrim. In service to Constantine's mother, Helena. She carries with her a proclamation that commands all Christians to be granted full rights throughout the empire."

A young voice called back, "The tribune Severus claims the edict is a lie!"

"Tomorrow I will bring with me a copy of Constantine's proclamation. I will leave it on the rock here. You will see the truth of my words for yourself. If there are believers among you, it is no longer necessary for you to hide your faith. The persecution of followers of Jesus is forbidden."

The spears continued to glint in the dull light. The wind died while he spoke, which meant his voice carried well. He wished he could think of some fine way to end his talk, but all he could think to say was, "The blessings of the Risen Lord upon you all."

He turned and walked back to where his men waited.

: CHAPTER 25 :

:

When Anthony returned to camp, he gathered with Helena and Macarius and recounted his meeting with the leper. As he spoke, Helena felt herself flooded with an immense sense of peace, a tidal wave that broke across her heart with such force that she heard herself say, "The fast is over."

Anthony broke off in mid-sentence. "My lady?"

Helena turned to where her ever-silent maid sat. "Would you prepare us a meal?"

Macarius asked, "Has the miracle arrived?"

"I have no idea." She said. "But I feel..."

"What?"

Yet there was no further need to speak. The words did not exist that could encompass the feeling inside her. As though the unseen door was open and light spilled into her world, and all she had to do was walk forward and enter the new realm.

They ate a gruel of boiled oats flavored with honey from hives found in the grove's far side. Helena thought it was the finest meal she had ever tasted. When they were done, Helena asked, "Do you intend to take supplies to the lepers still today?"

"If you do not object. Their need is very great."

"May I come with you?"

Every head in hearing range turned to stare at her. Anthony asked, "You wish to meet the leper girl?"

"I feel called to this. Why, I have no idea."

In the late afternoon light, Anthony and his men loaded six donkeys with provisions and water skins. They set off the hour before sunset. The same group of soldiers followed them down the slope. The same cluster of spears marked their progress from the city walls.

When the ragged figures emerged from the trees ahead, Anthony said, "Wait here."

Helena replied, "I want to help."

"My lady, it is not safe."

"Nothing about this journey has been safe. Not one step of my travels. And yet here I stand, protected by God. Please. Let me help."

The soldiers halted with evident relief. Helena and Anthony each took the reins of three donkeys and led them forward. Helena forced herself to show no reaction as the lepers off-loaded the supplies and carried them back to their camp.

Then the young woman came back to where Anthony and Helena stood.

Anthony offered her food from his own sack. Helena forced herself not to cringe as her rag-covered hand took his proffered meal. They waited as she ate.

Helena felt her heart ache from the glimpses beneath the woman's veil. She thought the woman was very young. Which only made the moment more tragic.

Helena settled upon a rock and motioned for the woman to do the same. "My name is Helena. What is your name?"

The woman pretended not to hear. Helena accepted the silent response to mean that the woman had given up everything when she was banished to this place, even her name. Helena tried once more. "How old are you?"

This time she answered. "A thousand years."

Helena fought down a sudden urge to weep. In the silence, Anthony began to speak. To Helena's astonishment, he told the woman of his wife. And how she had loved him and then left him bereft with her passage. And how on this voyage he had come to know a new depth of faith, one that had taken hold in the barren earth of his life and transformed not just his day, but his vision.

The woman did not respond. She made no sound whatsoever. Tears formed and fell, but she made no move to wipe them away. When Anthony stopped talking, Helena knew it was time. She said, "Last year my husband stole my life from me. He divorced me. He robbed me of the home I had made for us. He took my good name. He sent me away in disgrace. I thought my life was over. I thought I could never forgive him. I thought God had abandoned me. I thought...I thought it would be impossible to ever forgive God."

The woman covered her face with hands wrapped in filthy rags. The skin that was visible was grayish and flakey, like the mold that grew on stale bread. Helena swallowed hard and continued, "The Lord called me to take this journey. I thought it was to either die upon the road or complete a quest for him, and all the while I thought I was unworthy, because in my secret heart I burned with bitter rage over how God had let me be treated by life. Others might think me a saint. But I knew just how unworthy I was. How I lied with every step. How I failed him with every breath."

The woman moaned softly. She might have fashioned the word *stop*. But Helena could not be certain. So she continued, "Of all the many miracles I have witnessed in Judea, the greatest is the healing of my own heart. That is what has brought my friend and me to sit with you this evening. To share with you the power that Jesus offers. The chance to know his love and peace. Even here, in the valley of sorrow and despair. He calls to you, as he has called to us."

"Amen," Anthony said softly. "Amen."

Still the woman did not speak. Helena motioned to Anthony, and together they rose and started back to where the soldiers waited. Further on, the wall was rimmed by soldiers. Their spears glinted in the day's final light. Only then did Helena realize what a rich prize she made, standing here in the desolate valley. Only then did she think of the silent power that kept her protected. Only then.

As they started up the rise to the Mount of Olives, Helena turned back to find the leper still standing there. The young woman called out after them, "I think I am nineteen."

: CHAPTER 26 :

:

Anthony dreamed of the young woman, turned old by illness and all the sharp edges that life had used to cut away her world. He woke still hearing her call after them, the young-old voice singing a dirge by just speaking her age. He was so caught up in the memory that it took him a moment to realize a trio of soldiers marched toward his bedroll.

"Sire, are you awake?"

"Barely." Anthony scrambled to his feet and accepted the steaming mug from Cratus. "How went the night?"

"Quiet, sire. Very quiet. But there's something you should see."

Anthony followed the grizzled sergeant to where Favian and Evander stood by the edge of the grove. He stared down the road and saw that a troop of some twenty soldiers was leaving Jerusalem by the shattered gate. They headed down the road toward the Olive Mount. And at their head walked an officer whose burnished breastplate shone in the morning light.

The appearance of the squad caught Anthony by surprise. Evidently Favian shared his puzzlement, for he demanded, "Severus approaches us under a banner of truce?"

"It seems so."

Evander grunted his disbelief. "The man has never offered anything to believers save his blade."

Cratus nodded. "It would not be the first time a scouting team had been sent out under a flag of truce."

Anthony found it difficult to focus upon the apparent danger, as though more than the dream's lingering images held him from seeing clearly. "Let's go see."

Cratus demanded, "Should I wake Helena?"

"This is a soldier's duty. Let her sleep."

The day was made for astonishments, for as the officers started down the hill, two rabbis came racing over, their black robes caught up in one hand so as to keep them from tumbling. Several of the soldiers took that as a sign and started forward as well. When it looked as though the entire camp was about to empty, Anthony raised his hand and said, "These first dozen, come with us. The rest of you, stay where you are." He gestured to the rabbis. "You may join us also, if you will."

Severus stood at the forefront, his face twisted in the same snarl Anthony had last seen from the back of a horse, bearing down on their oasis. Anthony found himself utterly removed from the man's ire. They reached the valley floor and started up the rise. As an officer, he should have disliked how he had to climb up to meet Severus. It put him at a tactical disadvantage. When he was three paces from their enemy, Anthony stopped and said, "What do you want, Severus?"

"Lord Severus to you, scum. You are commanded to bow before your betters."

"I always do."

"Salute, then. For you stand before a tribune."

"As do you."

Their foe disliked that immensely. "The upstart mother of a failed officer should give thanks that I allow her the chance to greet another dawn."

"She gives thanks constantly, but not to you." It seemed to him as though a wall had been erected about his senses. One that could not even be assailed by the enemy's wrath. "And her son has never been defeated in battle."

"*Yet*," Severus snarled. "Never been defeated yet."

"I asked you what you wanted."

Beneath his gleaming breastplate, Severus wore a parade uniform. His leather armbands were emblazoned with Roman eagles, the shoulders embossed with gold leaf. His helmet glinted in the light. His crimson robe was held in place with gold epaulets, the symbol of royal standing. He took in Anthony's gray homespun, and a sneer split his oiled beard. "Did she demand you dress like the scum you lead?"

"They are not scum, and the lady has made no demand."

Anthony's calm only heightened his rage. "What is the purpose of your coming to Aelia Capitolina?"

"The same as when we spoke in Caesarea. We accompany the lady Helena to *Jerusalem*. On pilgrimage. And to deliver a message." Anthony lifted his voice so that it carried to the rearmost soldier. "The Edict of Milan declares all Christians to be full citizens of Rome. All persecutions are hereby—"

"The caesar of Damascus repudiates this so-called edict!"

"Maximinus is no longer caesar of Damascus and has no power to repudiate anything. The *caesar* of the Eastern Empire has placed his signature upon the document. Along with Constantine."

Severus started to protest further, but one of his men said, "Sire, there is enemy movement upon the mount."

Severus lifted his glare and snarled, "We stand beneath the banner of truce!"

Anthony turned to discover his voice had carried further than he expected, at least the tone, for a mass of soldiers were gathering at the border of the trees, their weapons drawn and shields at the ready. Anthony called out, "Sheath your weapons! Come no closer!" He did not turn back until he was certain his orders were obeyed. He directed his words to the young officer behind Severus. "We are not your enemies. All are welcome to join us beneath the Lord's banner."

Severus barked, "You are hereby ordered to return the deserters to their posts."

"There are no deserters among us."

"We lost seventy-six troopers during the night!"

"And more I hope will join us tonight," Anthony replied. "You among them, God willing."

"They are deserters, and they will be crucified like their so-called prophet."

"Jesus was no prophet. He was the Risen Lord."

"He was nothing!" Severus swiped the air between them, as though guiding a blade into Anthony's throat. "Look at you. A Roman officer consorting with rabble, dressed like a slave, guarding a shamed innkeeper's daughter! You disgrace your corps!"

Anthony decided there was nothing to be gained from arguing. "Vacate the area known as the Temple Mount. Remove your soldiers from this side of the city. Accept the Edict of Milan." He glanced to where the young rabbi observed everything with glittering black eyes. "And make Judeans welcome in Jerusalem once more."

"Aelia Capitolina is and always will be a Roman city!"

"*Jerusalem* was a Judean city before Rome was even named. It is theirs still."

"You offer what in exchange?"

Anthony knew Severus expected negotiations to begin now. Instead, he turned away and signaled for his men to return up the hill. "Deliver the message."

CHAPTER 27

For the rest of that day, the rabbis stood at the fringe of the expanding camp and observed and muttered. Helena was impatient, but she did not speak. Instead, she settled herself upon a stone and read from the Psalms. After the noon meal, the rabbis approached her. When they saw what she studied, they departed. She had no choice but wait, and pray. Either the rabbis would choose to help them, or they would not.

Toward sunset, she and Anthony again loaded up a pair of donkeys with supplies and started down the road leading to the valley floor. A cluster of soldiers and even a few civilians accompanied him. The soldiers manning the city wall watched their descent into the valley.

As they turned off the main road and started toward the grove of desert pines, Helena heard the clomp of hooves. Macarius urged a donkey toward them and called cheerfully, "Might I join you?"

"You'll miss the evening service."

He waved carelessly. "They will be well served without me. There are half a dozen priests among the newcomers."

"I didn't know that."

"Why should you bother with such things when you have thousands of souls to attend to?" He reached to Anthony. "Help me down."

Helena said, "The terrain is rough from here to the camp. You should ride."

"I should do many things. But I have sat all the day long, listening to the rabbis argue among themselves. Whether or not they should help us, whether they indeed know the route our Lord took to his death and our salvation. Whether they can name the hill of crucifixion." He gripped the staff and limped forward but did not let go of Anthony's arm. "I suspect they know, but they treat knowledge like silver. It is all our armies have left them, their knowledge of the holy texts."

"We could do this without their help," Anthony said.

"We could also get it all very wrong," Helena replied.

"We need them desperately," Macarius agreed. "For we have no other way of knowing which hill was the one upon which our Lord hung and died and paved our way to heaven."

The young woman stepped alone from the grove's shadows. Helena's heart went out to her. The woman held herself in a permanent bow, as though constantly expecting another blow. Helena said to the priest, "Perhaps you should stay here."

"I shall do no such thing," Macarius replied. He lifted his voice and called, "The Lord's blessings upon you, child. May I approach?"

Her only response was to glance fearfully at Helena, who said, "Macarius is a friend."

"Indeed I am, and I would like to be your friend as well."

Together they drew the donkeys forward. Others emerged from the grove, off-loaded the supplies, and departed. All without speaking a word.

When all but the young woman were gone, Macarius asked, "Might I ask your name, child?"

Helena assumed she would not answer. But the young woman hesitated a long moment before whispering, "Aquilina."

"Ah, the ancient name for an eagle. How perfect. May your heart ever soar upward to its eternal resting place." He spoke with the same lighthearted tone he used in addressing everyone. "Tell me, my child, do you know the name of Jesus?"

The rag-covered hand pointed at Anthony. "He told me. And then the lady did as well."

Macarius showed great delight. "Did they, indeed. How marvelous. Would you care to pray with us, my dear?"

She might have nodded, or it could have been a shiver. But it was enough for Macarius. The priest gave Anthony his staff and settled his hand upon her head and spoke gently, "May our Lord Jesus Christ shelter you in his loving embrace. May his peace surround you and shield you. May you know his love. In your darkest hour, may his light illuminate your heart and your way forward. Amen."

Helena stepped forward and placed her hand beside Macarius. "In the name of the Risen One, amen."

Helena and Macarius walked the young woman back into the leper's camp, while Anthony followed, pulling on the donkeys' reins. The other figures flitted back into the trees and made no attempt to come closer as Macarius offered them the sign of peace. When Macarius was done, Anthony helped him climb back onto the donkey. Together they bade the young woman a heartfelt farewell.

They were almost back to the road when Macarius said to Anthony, "You gave witness to Aquilina?"

"The words came to me unbidden," he replied. "I heard myself speak of my wife, my child, my loss, and my newfound hope."

Macarius reached over and settled his hand upon the officer's head. "I could not be prouder of you if I had named you at your birth."

: CHAPTER 28 :
:

The next morning, they awoke to discover the soldiers were gone.

Helena took her time wandering about the camp. She could see the officers talking gravely as they peered across the sunlit valley to Jerusalem's empty walls. Around mid-morning, they finally decided to send a foray across to survey the city. Helena watched as Favian and Cratus and Evander all argued fiercely for the honor.

They all waited and watched, even the rabbis, as Favian led his group of thirty men through the ancient gates. Two hours later, he returned to report that the entire western district had been emptied. Even so, Anthony inspected the city until the morning service, searching for any sign of deception.

Afterward, Helena approached him and asked, "Is it safe?"

"It appears so, my lady. But there is only one way to be certain."

"Then let us go."

As they started down the road, the camp emptied behind them. No invitation had been made, no commands given. But soldiers and former prisoners alike flooded the road. Some raced ahead, taking up stations at either side of the roadway. And they sang.

Very flesh, yet Spirit too,
Uncreated, and yet born
God and Man in One agreed
Truly life in death indeed,

Fruit of God and Mary's seed,
At once impassable and torn
By suffering here below
Jesus Christ, whom as our Lord we know.

They proceeded directly to the Temple Mount. The city's Roman inhabitants saw them coming, shuttered their shops, and cleared the streets. The temple to Saturn was empty. Only the smoldering incense stands gave testimony to the departed.

Helena stood upon the vast stone plaza and gazed at the edifice for a time. "Anthony."

"My lady."

"Tear this down."

"As you command." He turned to where Evander and Favian stood and asked, "Do I have volunteers for this duty?"

* * *

Helena spent her day observing as Anthony and his team began the destruction of the Roman temple. It would take weeks to clear away every last vestige. All she wanted was to announce their intention. Helena watched as the massive bronze incense burners and sacrificial urns were dumped over the wall and hoped this would be enough to bring the rabbis around.

Evander established a camp on a flat rubble-strewn terrain below the Temple compound. The city walls and a cluster of ruined structures formed an ideal perimeter. Their numbers had grown such that there were more than enough troops for both duties. And still more kept coming. Soldiers slipped through the ruins, casting fearful glances behind them. Helena did not need to hear their tales to know that Severus threatened to kill any who were caught trying to change sides.

A cliff of massive close-set stones rose up alongside their camp, forming one side of the Temple Mount. In the early afternoon, the rabbis clustered by these ancient stones. They settled striped cloths over their heads and faces and wrapped leather boxes to their forearms. They held ancient texts, and they swayed in disjointed unison. The entire camp was silenced by the sight.

When the rabbis stowed away their cloths and boxes, Helena walked over and addressed the youngest rabbi, "May I ask what you are doing?"

"We pray."

"Why here?"

The dark eyes glittered with four hundred years of bitter regret. "We do not know precisely how the Lord's Temple was positioned. We are forbidden from setting foot upon the Holy of Holies."

Helena understood. Other Romans had demolished their holy place. That was all the rabbi could see. And nothing she said or did would ever erase that stain. She bowed. "Thank you for your explanation."

After sunset, Helena climbed the rubble to stand upon the city wall. Anthony accompanied her and then went back to help Macarius pick his way across the rubble to stand alongside them. Moonlight bathed the city in a timeless pastel. The valley beyond the wall glowed an ethereal silver. In the distance, Helena spotted the small spring that normally supplied the lepers with water. Now all that remained was a circle of dried mud that gleamed in the moonlight. Helena thought of Aquilina and prayed that the young woman rested peacefully that night.

When Macarius glanced sorrowfully toward the city's highest hill, Helena asked, "Where was your church located?"

"There are remnants of a second wall within this one, my lady. It forms that dark line you see along the rise there. Within that boundary lies the city's oldest section. The lone house still standing, that is said to be where our Lord and his disciples held the last supper before his Crucifixion. Our church was nearby."

Anthony said, "There is nothing left?"

"Memories." Macarius replied. "Hope for tomorrow. On a night like this, the two are enough."

The air cooled swiftly, accompanied by a rising night wind. The breeze carried a distinct desert fragrance. Helena breathed the scent of desert flowers pressed by the sun and left hidden for a thousand years. Waiting.

She was a stranger here, and yet she felt divinely welcomed. She had come fearful of finding death but had discovered instead a genuine gladness for all that remained unseen beyond the bend of time. To know the joy found in service, in awaiting the gift of another dawn.

As she picked her way down from the wall, she confessed, "I have been thinking of Aquilina."

"As have I," Anthony replied. "And my wife and child."

"Do you miss them?"

"With every breath. And yet I have found a joy in tomorrow and all the days beyond that." He hesitated and then added, "I feel guilty over knowing such joy."

"You shouldn't."

"My mind knows this. I tell myself I have every right to know happiness."

"But it is hard to turn away from sorrow," Helena agreed.

"It is like the river of my life is being set upon a new course." Anthony turned back to the unseen valley. "Have you noticed how Aquilina keeps standing there, long after we leave?"

"The image comes to me in my dreams."

"I wonder how long it's been since the last time she heard a kind word or a caring voice."

"You are a good man, Anthony," Helena said. "I am glad you are here."

"As am I, my lady." But he kept his face turned toward the moonlight and the city wall.

"What is it?"

"Perhaps here is the only logic to be found in loss," he replied. "How it grants me the ability to speak to another's grief and offer hope to another wounded soul. And help them lift their gaze from the lure of a grave that is not yet theirs to claim."

: CHAPTER 29 :

:

The next morning, the rabbis agreed to assist them. The elder rabbi personally informed them of this decision. Together with the entire camp, they walked empty lanes, crossed the city, and halted at a rubble-strewn hilltop beside the city's eastern boundary wall. The gray-bearded teacher announced, "This was Pilate's palace."

The place was a field of ruin. Helena knew the governor's palace had been famed for its gardens. The royal chambers would have been opulent and vast. Here there was nothing save weeds. She surveyed the destruction and asked, "Can this be?"

The elder was definite. "Our records on the holy city stretch back three thousand years. There can be no question." He pointed one ancient hand. "When the Zealots overran the Roman garrison and took control of the city, the first building they destroyed was Herod's palace, the second was Pilate's. After our defeat, this one was rebuilt. When we retook the city seventy years later, we destroyed it again. This time, they did not rebuild."

Helena nodded acceptance. "And the road? And the hill?"

"Pilate's seat of judgment was the forecourt to his estate." The elder pointed down a long sloping avenue. "This is the most direct route from the palace to Golgotha."

In the distance rose a second temple, not so grand as the one that had occupied the Temple compound, and much newer. Helena turned to where the priest stood and asked, "Macarius, what is that structure?"

"A temple to Venus, my lady." He limped over to join them. "Completed only last season and not yet dedicated."

She asked the rabbi, "You are certain that was the place of crucifixion?"

"There can be no question."

She bowed. "I and all who shall follow in my footsteps thank you."

The elder had the good grace to bow in response. Helena waited until the rabbis' footsteps dwindled into the distance and then said, "Macarius."

From the back of his donkey, the priest responded, "My lady."

"From this day forward, this road shall be known as the *Via Dolorosa*."

The name meant, "The Way of Grief and Suffering." Macarius bowed low upon his saddle, granting her words a solemn formality. "It shall be as you say, my lady."

She turned and stared down the road. But before she took her first step, voices began singing behind her.

Helena turned to them. She did not speak. But the message was clear enough. The song ended on a faltering note.

She allowed the silence to hang over them for a time and then said, "Let us begin."

* * *

Anthony had marched at the forefront of half a dozen armies, into almost a hundred different engagements. He had known the raw, heart-pounding fear of approaching a larger force who occupied a fortified position. He had heard the rush of steel-tipped death aimed straight at him. He had lived through countless sweat-drenched nights, worried over himself and his men. He had carried the impossible weight of his dead infant son to the waiting grave.

But nothing in his experience approached the glorious dread of this walk.

The sun pierced the gray veil in places, lancing the city and the stone lane with intense light. Jerusalem appeared to be empty. The shops were shuttered, the inhabitants gone. Helena and her company walked in utter silence. The loudest sound was their footsteps and the occasional broken sob.

Anthony could well understand the weeping. He did not simply follow the path taken by Jesus. He carried his own cross as well. He had never felt so bound to his sins, his failings, or his absent wife and child. All the impossible burdens of life, all the miserable flaws. He was not merely laden with woe and guilt. He was convicted. He deserved to die.

The road dipped down into a city vale and then began to climb. The way became segmented, with broad central steps separating two shallow stone grooves in which wheels could ride. Up ahead, a blade of sunlight fell upon the unfinished temple, and it seemed as though the stone edifice melted away. Leaving a hill of death. Waiting for them all.

They climbed to the crest and halted at the temple steps. The light faded as the clouds again veiled the sky. The pillars supported a roof, but the walls were not in place. At its center was the altar and a marble statue depicting Venus.

Anthony knew without being told that Helena waited for him to act. He turned and found Favian and Evander at the forefront of the massive assembly that followed them. Both their faces were wet. As was his own. He silently motioned to them. They were instantly joined by a score of men and more besides.

Soldiers and former prisoners together bent to the task of dismantling the altar with their bare hands. They then took down the statue and carried it to the rear of the temple. Anthony discovered he was directly above the valley and the pine grove. He and the others cast the statue over the edge. As he watched it tumble down the rocky ridge, he saw a figure emerge from the grove. The person was too far away for him to see through the shroud covering her head, but he knew it was Aquilina.

Behind him, Helena said, "Macarius, assist me."

The wounded pastor's voice was raw with emotion. "My lady, I am yours to command."

"I wish to rededicate this temple to the Lord our God."

"Mistress, in the eyes of God and man, the deed is already done."

: CHAPTER 30 :

:

Helena stood and watched as soldiers and villagers and former prisoners alike all joined together and tore the temple's ornamental trappings out by their roots. The only person who was apparently not fixated on the process was Anthony. She walked over to stand beside him. "Is something the matter?"

"Look down there."

She peered over the steep ledge. The hillside back toward the city was a gentle slope, lined by the road. But in this direction the heights fell away steeply. Far to the right was the tiny spring and the grove of ancient pines. Directly below them stood a lonely figure. "Is that Aquilina?"

"It is. And she's waving to us."

"Do you think she wants to come up?"

"Actually, my lady, I think it's the other way around."

"But we are busy doing..." Helena studied the surrounding cliff. The road leading from Jerusalem to the Mount of Olives was on the other side of the grove from where they now stood. She had never seen the valley from this angle. Something about the way the sunlight cast shadows caught her attention. "Are those caves?"

"It appears so," Anthony replied.

The longer she looked, the more certain she was of what she saw. The valley was narrow here, perhaps three hundred paces across. The cliff face was pockmarked with hundreds of small openings. "Those caves were fashioned by man."

"They are crypts," Anthony agreed. "We stand upon an ancient burial valley."

Helena saw as Aquilina again beckoned to them. Behind them, Macarius said, "Brothers and sisters, we are gathered here in wonder at the impossible sacrifice made real."

Helena turned and motioned to the priest. "Forgive me. Could you wait just a moment, please?"

"Of course, my lady."

"Thank you." Helena turned to Anthony and said, "Go see what she wants."

Anthony must have felt the same urgency, for without a word or backward glance he dropped over the ledge.

* * *

Anthony descended by way of a narrow trail that was little more than a goat path. He took his time, moving carefully, for the way was steep. To his surprise, the young woman started up toward him.

Dozens and dozens of circular openings dotted the lower ridge face. Many were covered with rocks carved flat as millstones and set in narrow grooves. He knew the trail he took had once been used by gravediggers and families in mourning.

A wretched year of affliction had brought him back to the same place from which he had started. His life had ended at the border of one grave, and by another, it was to begin anew. Anthony did not know how he knew this. But he had never been more certain of anything in his entire life. He would have wept, but his shock was so great he could not muster tears.

Aquilina climbed up to stand just below his own position. She pointed at a hole where the stone had been rolled away and said in a voice soft as the breeze blowing down the valley of death. "There is wood in here that will not burn."

* * *

Helena started moving before Anthony finished reporting what
Aquilina had said. Her pace was only slowed by the need to help
Macarius climb back upon the donkey. When the priest would not
move fast enough to suit her, she bodily shoved him up. He might
have objected, had she waited long enough for him to speak. But
as soon as he was up, she gripped the reins and started running.

Where the road dipped to its lowest point before climbing back
up toward Pilate's palace, a trio of ruined structures formed a
rubble field that joined with an opening in the city wall. Helena
scrambled through the ruins, tugging at the donkey's reins and
ignoring the animal's protests. When she passed through the wall
and scrambled down the embankment, she set off running as fast
as she had in her life. She felt as though the winds of an entire
world pushed her on.

Behind her, the crowd of people rushed to catch up. The oldest
and sickest were strung out far behind them, almost back to
the hill of sorrows. She finally arrived where Anthony stood, so
breathless she staggered and used the mule to keep her upright.

A number of the others had taken the more direct route down
the cliff face. She saw them cluster about one particular opening
and willed herself not to weep. She wanted to remember every
instant of this. She wanted to see it all with crystal clarity. She
wanted the sight etched upon her eternal soul. Where it belonged.

"An elder in my church once told me that wood drenched
in human blood is resistant to fire." Macarius spoke with soft
reverence. "It becomes cured such that the stench is said to bring
terrible nightmares."

The pine grove and the leper camp were both empty now. Only
Aquilina, who remained standing in the trees' shade, observing it
all.

"The Romans used their crucifixes over and over," Macarius
went on. "Such wood naturally carries a terrible dread."

Helena found herself very grateful for the old pastor's voice, for it kept her from being overwhelmed by it all. She waited as Anthony scrambled down the trail and then said, "Describe for me exactly what you saw."

He pointed back up the ridge, to the tomb surrounded by many of their company. "The rock was rolled back. Inside, six pieces of wood are laid out like bodies."

Helena said, "Show me, please."

"Follow me, my lady." As they started up the track, Anthony lifted his voice and ordered, "Everyone else remain here! The trail is too narrow for us all. Those of you up there, move away and give the empress room. Cratus, block off the trail!"

Helena clambered up the narrow path. Evander and Favian formed an honor guard, standing to either side of the cave's mouth. Anthony held back as she lowered her head and looked inside.

The cave was cool, the air tasting of dried herbs and dust. Helena remained in the opening for a long moment. Then she entered the cave and felt a tremor race through her.

The cave was carved in the traditional fashion. A broad shelf was shaped from the rock, intended to hold the bodies of an entire clan. Across from this was fashioned a narrow bench, where mourners could sit and keep vigil.

Only, this particular grave held neither bodies nor bones. Instead, six lengths of wood were laid out upon the empty stone berth. Three tall stanchions and three cross-ties. Each piece was as thick as her waist. The wood was black.

Above the wood, set upon a tiny ledge where an oil lamp had perhaps once burned, was a single strip of wood.

The wood was the size of Helena's two hands. Burned into the surface were Roman letters.

It was a common practice through the Roman empire to label

the crucifixes of the worst criminals. Signs would be nailed into the cross above their heads, with the crimes branded into the wood.

Upon this wood were inscribed four letters, signifying not a crime, but a mockery. Pilate had not wanted to condemn the man whom he had found innocent, but he had been forced by the Sanhedrin, the Temple council. The sign read, *Jesus of Nazareth, the King of the Jews.*

*   *   *

They lay the wood out as crosses upon the valley floor. They could tell which cross-tie went where by lining up the nail holes. The sign's placement, however, was a mystery. Perhaps it had been lashed to the top or held with a small nail. In any case, they had no idea which cross had held the Messiah.

The people crowded in a great circle around the three crosses laid there upon the rocky earth. A crow gave off its coppery song. The breeze sighed through the pine grove behind them.

Waiting.

Helena turned and searched. Anthony turned with her. The crowd was massive and so compressed they were fashioned into a great and silent union. They waited with her. They knew they witnessed something beyond earthly comprehension. They were content to stand or kneel and partake of hours beyond the reach of man or time.

"What we need," Helena said, "is a sign."

Macarius stood beside her. He leaned upon his staff and waited with the rest of them.

She turned to the scarred priest and suggested, "Macarius, touch the wood. See if the Lord will heal you."

"Mistress, I dare not." He smiled sadly. "These are my thorns. They are there for a purpose. I am wounded so that I might lead my injured flock."

"You are certain?"

"I prayed," Macarius replied. "Many times. The Lord has answered."

She did not like it, though she had no choice but accept. She searched the crowd. There were many injured among them. Yet none stepped forward.

Waiting.

Then the hand of God touched her.

The sense of being joined to the unseen was undeniable. The impact was as vivid as during her vision. Only now she stood with eyes open, surrounded by a multitude.

The Spirit rested upon her. The gift was so intense Helena felt tears spring unbidden from her eyes, as though the emotions demanded some release.

*   *   *

Anthony saw the change come upon Helena. Whatever question he might have had was erased that same instant, for he felt the hand of God touch him as well. Though he had never experienced anything like this before, the moment held an unmistakable force. He heard the Spirit's unspoken word.

In that same instant, Anthony realized he would never leave Judea. This was to be his home. The crowd of soldiers who surrounded him were his to command. And their task was to serve the community of believers. In the face of danger and human wolves who had ravaged them for centuries, Anthony and his men would establish order and safety. They would rebuild the razed churches and reform the demolished communities. They would serve, and he would live out a sheaf of days filled with meaning. And when his time on earth was ended, he would leave behind a different world.

And in that moment of joyful acceptance, Anthony was granted a second message.

So that he knew this was indeed God's finger resting upon his heart, pointing out the direction to the remainder of his life, he would be given a sign.

And when he realized what that sign was to be, it was all he could do not to fall crashing to his knees.

"Anthony?"

"My lady." He faltered. He forced himself to swallow hard and say, "God has spoken to me."

"And to me as well." She held out her hand. "Let us do this together."

The crowd parted. Together they walked back toward the grove. Soldier and empress, widower and disgraced daughter of a forgotten innkeeper, heeding a word that was not heard by human ears. They had been joined at a moment when they were alone and afraid and destined to perish. Now they were joined upon the pilgrim's road, surrounded by a thousand wasted lives brought to new hope by the invisible road they shared. Drawn to the one true and eternal destination.

The scrape of feet and staff signaled another coming up beside him. "May I join you?"

Anthony found himself unable to speak. Helena, however, was made of sterner stuff. "Come, my dear friend. Let us go to her together."

The injured priest and the broken soldier and the lady with no name continued forward. They passed through the avenue lined by silent friends, over to where the young woman sat upon the log beneath the whispering pines.

"No," she whimpered.

Anthony could not see more than her form, but it did not matter. She shimmered and shone with the promise of God's presence. He said simply, "Come."

"Unclean," she whimpered. "Forbidden."

Helena reached forward and softly urged, "Child, take my hand."

"Do as she says, dear one," Macarius said. "All is well."

The rags covering her fingers fashioned into a smooth glove that fit into Helena's grasp. Together they returned to the center of the silent circle.

Helena smiled and asked, "Daughter, are you a follower of Jesus?"

"I am," she whispered. "If he will have me."

Helena pointed to the three crosses laid in the yellow dust. "Touch the wood."

It was when she knelt before the central cross that it happened. The silent chorus of heavenly joy, the erasing of the veil that covered the valley and the world beyond. The light was blinding.

The young woman gave a cry of wonder. "I am healed!"

: CHAPTER 31 :

:

The soldiers stood in silent ranks. Waiting. Anthony, tribune of the new Judean regiment, stood at their fore. An opening split their ranks from the road leading to the arena to the ship moored at the harbor wall. The hills of Caesarea rose around them. The day was blisteringly hot. Anthony found the scene astonishingly similar to the day when they had first arrived. And yet everything had changed.

Cratus, head of Helena's personal guard, stepped from the shadows and signaled. Anthony turned to the two men flanking him and said, "I will inspect the troops."

Favian, newly appointed leader of the scouts regiment, saluted. Evander, Anthony's second in command, wheeled about and bellowed, "Troop, attention!"

Nine hundred and eighteen right sandals stamped the harbor stones. Anthony walked their ranks because the men deserved this accolade. The soldiers had been gathered from legions through the surrounding lands. They were a motley assortment of clans and cultures. United by the same impossible gift that granted Anthony the strength to lead them. He paused by one of their most recent volunteers, a former jailer from the arena, a disgraced trooper named Ianius. Anthony greeted him with a hand on his shoulder and was rewarded with a huff of surprise. It was hardly a common gesture between commanding officer and new recruit. But theirs was a singular legion in many respects.

The armies formerly guarding the Judean lands had vanished. Severus had not been seen since the day they entered Jerusalem. Anthony needed more men. Judea had formerly been guarded by two full legions. If their enemies in Damascus chose this moment to attack, they would be overwhelmed. But he found himself unable to worry, and counted this as a sign of the new season. Their God would provide.

When he had passed before the last of his men, Anthony returned to the fore and nodded to Evander, who shouted, "Parade rest!"

"The table," Anthony ordered.

"Sir!" Evander and his second stepped to the side of their troop and drew forth a scarred table they had found in the bowels of the arena. The wood was stained and pitted. They could have selected one of the polished fixtures from the neighboring governor's palace, as Firmilian and his entire troupe had fled to Damascus. But Anthony had decided this item, taken from the place where so many of his brethren had ended their earthly days, was more fitting.

Then they waited.

To their right, arrayed along the harbor wall, amassed a crowd of worshippers. Many were former prisoners. Others came from the villages they had helped rebuild. Aquilina stood in the front ranks, a lovely testament to the time of miracles. And of hope for a new tomorrow. Anthony felt her eyes upon him but forced himself to focus upon the road. Waiting with his troops.

The Roman capital of Judea was completely silent. The temples that crowned the surrounding hills were empty, as were the streets and markets and forts and harbor. The lone sound came from a gull circling overhead.

Then he heard the scrape of footsteps.

Before he could signal, Evander bellowed for the legion to come to attention.

Helena was the first to appear. The woman in gray looked exhausted, which was hardly a surprise. Since leaving Jerusalem, she had traveled the length and breadth of this realm, sharing the news of her son's edict, settling disputes over land and title among the survivors, and planting churches.

She was followed by Cratus, who led the donkey carrying the bishop of Jerusalem. Macarius offered a silent benediction to all.

Six soldiers followed, carrying a portion of the cross. Most of the wood was to remain at the church Macarius was to lead, there upon the mount of Golgotha. But Helena was taking one segment back with her to adorn the central altar of the new church she intended to establish in Rome. And from which she hoped to spread the good news throughout the empire.

No sign was given, for none was required. The legion of Judea dropped to their knees.

As usual, the soldiers carrying the cross had been selected at random from the ranks. It had been so throughout their sixty-day journey. Any officer who wished to serve at this duty was first required to strip away all rank and emblem. Each village through which they had passed had been invited to take part.

They settled the wood upon the scarred table and joined the ranks of their fellows. Macarius descended from his donkey and made his way to the table.

As was required at every such gathering, Anthony ordered quietly, "The troops will rise."

Macarius then declared, "We are gathered to bid our lady farewell and give thanks to the One who joins us. Our bonds cannot be severed by time nor distance. Those who are no longer named among the breathing, those who have gone before us into eternal glory, they join with us also."

The bishop led them all through the Eucharist. Helena held one cup, Anthony and Macarius the others. The silent procession took them through the heat of the day.

When they were done, Helena stepped before them and said, "I arrived at this very spot a broken woman. My life was over. And yet God had called me to make this journey. I cast aside everything I had left and came as a pilgrim. I came inviting the end. It was the only component of God's call that held any value—that I might arrive here and be defeated and breathe my last."

Anthony found himself unable to see the woman any longer. In her place was a blur of light and form, a gray figure at its heart, one who seemed only partly bound to the stones.

Helena went on, "God has led me to this point. Remaining just beyond my sight and reach, beckoning me forward, calling me to serve him one more day."

She surveyed their silent ranks for a long moment and then finished, "I thank you for your friendship and your support. And I urge you, too, to serve God each day"

Helena embraced Macarius, then Anthony, Evander, and Favian. She turned to the ship. Anthony realized the two men flanking him were incapable of speech, so he called for them, "Troop, salute!"

Helena started up the gangplank, a simple woman in gray. She returned the skipper's greeting and moved with Cratus and her maid to the stern railing. She remained there as the ship released its lines and raised sails and slipped away.

When the vessel had dissolved into the golden-hued distance, Anthony felt a hand come to rest upon his shoulder and discovered that Macarius had stepped up beside him. The bishop offered a confident smile and said, "And so it begins."

: EPILOGUE :

:

When Helena's ship departed from Caesarea, she left behind a nation transformed. Judeans were once again permitted to reside in their beloved city, which had been renamed Jerusalem. A new legion had been established, only the second army in all Roman history to welcome Christians. Their primary aim was to protect the lives of believers.

Helena left behind ninety-six churches she had planted over the length and breadth of Judea.

When she arrived in Cyprus, Helena discovered that the provincial capital had been destroyed only a few weeks earlier by a massive earthquake. Over half the province's population had been killed or maimed. Helena spent two years supervising the city's rebuilding. She spent all her remaining gold in the process.

The city fathers wanted to rename their city in her honor. Helena refused, saying such tributes were not proper for a simple pilgrim.

Instead, she asked that ships be made available for a sacred purpose. She segmented parts of the cross and dispatched them to the main cathedrals throughout the Roman Empire. A letter included with each explained her aim: to bind the empire together beneath the banner of shared faith and salvation.

When Helena left Cyprus to join her son in Rome, she traveled home wearing her pilgrim's robe.